MR.
GARDINER
and the
GOVERNESS

MR. GARDINER
and the
GOVERNESS

CLAIRVOIR CASTLE *Romances*
BOOK ONE

SALLY BRITTON

To K.M. Shea, W.R. Gingell, and Shari L. Tapscott

*Your books got me through COVID-19
and the misery of the year 2020.*

*Thank you for creating new worlds and strong heroines,
thank you for fairy-tales, and thank you for the gentle love stories.*

CHAPTER 1

MAY 1818

For most of Alice Sharpe's life, her relatives passed her from one home to another, the same way one might pass an unwanted family heirloom with little more value than sentiment. As she stood on the fine Persian rug before Her Grace, Sarah, the Dowager Duchess of Montfort, Alice reflected that this was the first time she had been given up to someone not even a part of the family.

"You do not look like a governess." The dowager duchess narrowed her eyes, the surrounding wrinkles deepening somewhat. She and Alice's great-aunt had served Queen Charlotte together as ladies-in-waiting, years before. "But Lucinda says you are well-suited to the position."

Alice swiftly lowered her gaze to the floor rather than be caught staring. "My great-aunt paid for much of my education herself, madam. I am four-and-twenty, and I have acted as a governess in all but name to several of my cousins for half a dozen years."

The dowager turned to the only other person in the room, her daughter-in-law, the current Duchess of Montfort. "What do you think, Cecilia?"

Her Grace, the Duchess of Montfort, made a thoughtful humming sound before she spoke, her beautiful voice low and cultured. "I think Miss Sharpe would do well here. She is old enough to keep the girls in check and has more than enough experience. It certainly helps that she is familiar with our set. Why has your great-aunt sent you here, rather than retain you as a companion or governess for someone in your family?"

The exotic flowers swirling upon the carpet provided no reassurance, but Alice followed their lines with her eyes as she spoke. "If it pleases Your Grace, my great-aunt learned of your need for a governess and thought there could be no greater honor than for me to serve in your household."

That was the reason Alice had been told, but she had heard the quiet conversations from the other end of the dinner table and the corners of drawing rooms. The family had tired of looking after her, and several of them thought Alice ought to make her own way in the world. At least until she was old enough not to compete with their daughters when suitors came to call.

Apparently, her fair hair and blue eyes made her a competitor for the interest of gentlemen bachelors.

Her unconscious place as a rival led to the three hour carriage ride that brought her to the castle, her trunks waiting in some unknown hall to either be swept up to some small bedchamber reserved for a governess or else tucked back into the carriage with her, sent back to her great-aunt in disgrace.

Though the duchess must know she was one of the most powerful women in England, she spoke with a gentleness Alice had not expected. "You would not oversee all the instruction for my daughters' education, of course. We bring in masters for riding, dancing, music, and art. I would expect you to see to their academic studies, and mind that they practiced everything else. You are to ensure they keep to their schedules. Is that agreeable to you, Miss Sharpe?"

"Your Grace, I am confident in my teaching abilities. I will make certain your daughters are well prepared to leave the school-room when you see fit. It would be an honor to serve you here at Clairvoir Castle."

Had Alice's great-aunt not pronounced the name of ancient lands as "Clee-ver," Alice certainly would have said it wrong. Despite the estate name being originally from the French, the early English inhabitants of the estate had corrupted the pronunciation hundreds of years before.

The duchess lowered her voice to speak to her mother-in-law, their quiet whispers the only sound in the large sitting room awash in the afternoon sunlight.

Alice's fingers twitched with the need to push her wired spectacles up her nose, but instead she gripped her skirts tighter. She needed the spectacles to read but could do without them otherwise. Yet her great-aunt had insisted she wear them as often as possible, as "Society considers girls wearing spectacles plain." Yet another way to ensure she did not distract her cousins' suitors.

Even at that moment, surrounded by crystal chandeliers, plush furnishings, and the rich tapestries of the newly rebuilt Castle Clairvoir, Alice presented herself as no more than a brown smudge in the bright glittering world of wealth. She wore a dark brown gown with a cream-colored fichu to hide the smooth skin of her neck. Her hair she had pulled back, most severely, into an unattractive and severe twist. The ash-blonde curls that escaped the strict style might have framed her face prettily, if not for the spectacles.

"Miss Sharpe." The dowager duchess spoke, and Alice raised her eyes enough to acknowledge the salutation. "We have decided to take you on at the rate of one-hundred pounds per annum should you adhere to the rules of the household and uphold your promises of education for Lady Isabelle and Lady Rosalind, and you will see after Lord James until he goes away to school this winter."

Relief and dread mingled together in Alice's heart. They

would not turn her away, yet the weight of the new responsibility nearly made her sag to the floor. The Duke of Montfort had three daughters and two sons. Alice now stood responsible for the three youngest of his noble children, girls as likely to marry into royalty as they were to catch cold, and the younger son.

The eldest son, bearing the honorary title Earl of Farleigh, was not at home. Lady Josephine, the eldest daughter, had left the schoolroom years before.

Alice hardly said another word for the quarter of an hour that the dowager and the duchess laid out their expectations and rules for her. Her behavior was to be as firmly controlled as the subjects she taught the girls, though the more she nodded and promised, the more Alice's courage grew.

She had always been clever, and she had always enjoyed learning. Thanks to her need to adjust and fit into numerous households and families over the years, she knew herself to be personable as well.

I can do this, she told herself repeatedly during the last of the interview. When a maid came to show Alice to her room, Alice squared her shoulders like a good soldier and prepared for the first meeting with her charges.

Passing through the corridors of the castle, the maid rattled off which rooms they walked by and their purpose. The maid was well-acquainted with the house and had an air of superiority about herself that Society's matrons would be hard-pressed to match.

Alice smiled to herself. She might not be a princess of any sort, but what girl hadn't wished to live in a place as lovely as Clairvoir Castle? The libraries and gardens were the stuff of legend, the family with a history reaching back to their aid of William the Conqueror. Few women of Alice's lower birth would ever walk the grounds, let alone have access to the house and family.

The opportunity thrilled her, as did finally having a purpose.

And yet.

Her gaze wandered to the wide windows of the ballroom as they passed its open door. For a moment, her breath hitched. Dreams of dancing in such a room with a handsome partner were a thing of the past. They had to be.

Governesses were not permitted any sort of courtship. They were almost non-entities.

Swallowing back the bleak thought, Alice gave her full attention to the maid once more. She clasped her hands before her, feeling her father's ring on her thumb. Though it was beneath her glove, the ring's presence comforted her.

The schoolroom would be her domain. The ballroom was better forgotten.

CHAPTER 2

Although most would think it strange to see a grown gentleman laying prostrate in the grass, Rupert Gardiner regularly put himself in exactly that position. At the moment, the majority of his body was pressed into the newly mown grasses of His Grace's southern gardens.

With a sketchbook splayed open before him, Rupert made note of the colors he would need to render the object of his study in greater detail.

Once he had made the appropriate notations, Rupert slowly reached for the water-net he had repurposed for his work. Water-nets were primarily used to capture smaller creatures from stream beds, but with a little modification, they were perfect for catching insects such as the common blue damselfly in his sight.

Rupert hesitated, however, and considered the speed with which the damselfly normally darted through a garden. The net was likely his best chance at catching it, but he did have his net-forceps, too. Newly ordered from Paris, where the study of insects was more popular than in England, he had only used them on heartier species. Even though the pamphlet suggested the forceps were an excellent way to catch butterflies, he had yet to try them for that.

Better use the net, then.

First, he pushed his black hair out of his eyes. He ought to have it cut but forgot immediately about the issue the moment he accomplished the catch. Quickly and in another careful series of movements, he secured the blue damselfly in a small cage with muslin meshed sides.

The insect flitted about, knocking into the mesh, before settling on the leafed stem he had positioned inside.

Rupert turned his attention to where the damselfly had been hovering. The small pond with a fountain in its center had attracted numerous insects throughout the morning. Some appeared to dip into the water for no more than a drink, but the damselfly had appeared busy in an area between lily pads, drawing his notice.

He had captured a female. Rupert had watched, as awe-inspired as ever by the workings of nature, as the female now in his possession had mated, then gone beneath the water to lay her eggs. The male of the species had remained nearby until the female approached the surface again, at which point he lowered himself to the water to rescue her, for she seemed too tired to break the surface of the pond on her own.

Why would an insect behave in such a way? What in the nature of the male damselfly drove him to rescue the female after he had already achieved his purpose in passing on his lineage? Most would say insects, and all creeping things of the earth, had no morality. What would drive the male to act so, save a natural urge to continue the species?

He jotted down his musings, though he had no intention of including them in his current work.

The Duke of Montfort had requested a catalog of insects and flora of his gardens, filled with illustrations and basic scientific notations. It was a monumental work, and the nature of the project would be invaluable to future generations. It was precisely the type of publication the Royal Society of London would notice.

If Rupert could gain the attention of the Royal Society, and the approval of its members, there was every chance of attaining a fellowship. Perhaps he might even get his work published in the *Philosophical Transactions*.

He looked down into the mesh cage at his specimen, watching as the tired female crawled slowly up the stick. So simple a creature, yet, with such a vastly mysterious life, it could be the key to seeing his name printed in the same journal that published Isaac Newton.

Though only seven-and-twenty years of age, Rupert had dreamed of being published by the Royal Society's journal for nineteen years.

Rupert went to work studying the plants in the pond. The damselflies had a liking for the area, likely due to the lack of predators. There were no fish, ornamental or otherwise, in the water. Though a fountain poured into it, the fountain had plenty of lily pads and moss growing around its edges to keep certain parts dark and cool, even at the hottest part of the day.

Sketching in the plant life always slowed the process of discovery. As vital as plants were to the insects, he simply did not have the love for the greenery that he did for the mysterious creepers and crawlers of the world. Flowers and trees grew where they were planted, then fed and sheltered wildlife.

As lovely as pond fronds might be to one observing the scene, his time would be better spent elsewhere.

After making notations for colors and the paints he would need for the sketch, Rupert stood and stretched his arms overhead. It was then that he remembered he had cast off his coat. His valet often bemoaned the state of Rupert's coat and trousers, the knees and elbows of which he coated in mud quite regularly, crawling about in gardens to look beneath leaves and rocks. Today, it would be Rupert's shirtsleeves that were moaned over.

Rupert grinned to himself and cast about, looking for the missing item. He had removed it in something of a temper, when the close-cut fabric made it difficult to get into the position necessary for observation of the damselfly.

His hat had disappeared, too, though he didn't recall where that had gone. After a few minutes of work, he found his coat beneath a shrub and his hat laid atop it. A moment later, he had gathered all his things and went in the direction of the castle. Though he could have stayed at his home part of the time, sixteen miles away, being on the duke's property at all hours made some of his observations far easier.

He took the servants' stairs up to the guest quarters. Rupert doubted the duchess would appreciate the sight of him upon the grand staircase given the dried mud on his trousers. Likely most in the household would find disturbing the cages full of insects he took to his room for further study.

Already, two maids had been banned from cleaning Rupert's chambers. One had killed a large moth, while another broke into hysterics over the presence of a Raft Spider. According to Billings, Rupert's valet, the two maids now assigned to the room rushed in to take care of the bedclothes, cleaned out the ashes and laid a fire, then ran out without looking anywhere else.

Billings was waiting for Rupert when he entered his bedchamber.

"Mr. Gardiner." Billings held out his hands to take two of the cages, then he walked them to the empty shelves where they would wait for Rupert's closer scrutiny.

Though the valet had no personal love for the tiny creatures Rupert brought home, he had no fear of them, either. Rupert had specifically asked valet candidates, some four years ago, how they handled such things as free-roaming spiders, bees, and earthworms.

Billings had been the only man who gave a satisfactory answer when he had said, "As I would an unwanted guest. If they overstayed their welcome, I would show them out the door."

"Good afternoon, Billings. Any news to report?" Rupert put his equipment down on the desk, his eyes already searching for the silver tray with the post. He found it, and it was empty.

"No, sir. Nothing was in the morning post, and the household continues on as it has. Although I have heard that there is a new governess for the youngest three children. The maids are full of speculation about her." Billings had no qualms with sharing the gossip of servants, which made him excessively entertaining some evenings.

"New governess. Hm. I hope that will put an end to those three following me about in the gardens." Though Rupert had at first appreciated the curiosity of the children in regard to his studies, he quickly realized they had their own motivations for following him. Lady Isabelle, at fourteen, and her sister Lady Rosalind, at twelve, had been trying to flirt with him. They were precocious girls and—given the position their father held in the world—would one day take Society by storm. After his amusement with their juvenile attempts wore off, he tried to ignore them. Their younger brother, Lord James, was only eight. He had a vested interest in learning to capture spiders, presumably for nefarious purposes.

Unfortunately, as they were the children of a duke, Rupert could not tell them to toddle off and pester someone else. Instead, he tolerated them with tight-lipped smiles.

With a governess in the castle, the children's hours would be better filled.

"Would you like to change your clothing, sir?" Billings eyed Rupert's coat with barely concealed horror. "Or would you prefer to wait for the dinner hour?"

Rupert looked at the mantel clock. It was only just past three. Too early for dinner, but ridiculous to change into anything else.

"I suppose dinner clothing would be appropriate, but I'll forgo the coat for now. I have my drawings still to do."

"Yes, Mr. Gardiner." Billings went into the small antechamber that served as closet and bathing room for Rupert. Meanwhile, Rupert started shedding the mud-crusted garments. The day had proved fruitful, and he hoped the discussion with the duke on his observations would be satisfying.

CHAPTER 3

Alice's second day in the castle, her first morning as the governess, was *not* an unqualified success. In fact, she qualified it as a minor disaster. Her nerves were somewhat frayed by the live frogs Lord James had introduced during their morning recitations. The amphibians had not bothered her as much as the shrieking of the boy's older sisters.

Lady Isabelle and Lady Rosalind had enough power in their lungs to launch a British man-of-war out of a harbor. Returning the schoolroom to order afterward had taken time away from their study of geography.

"Lady Rosalind, will you kindly point out the location of India on the globe, please?" Alice had asked, ready to begin a lesson on that region.

Unfortunately, she learned at that point Lady Rosalind thought India a part of South America. The girl peered at the southern hemisphere for some time before asking, "Why isn't India labeled?"

Lady Isabelle had laughed at her sister before proudly spouting off the names of all the crown heads of Europe to prove herself superior.

That had caused another argument.

The art instructor staying in the castle sent word shortly after twelve that he was ready for the children's lessons. Alice sent them off, relieved beyond words to have an hour of quiet.

It was an hour she ought to spend organizing the schoolroom and preparing for the next lesson. Standing three floors above ground, looking out a window into the gardens, Alice yearned for something else.

The Clairvoir gardens were famous throughout England for their beauty. All of Society had sought news of how the duchess had rebuilt the castle in the past decade, and everyone sought to copy Her Grace. Even Alice, living on the fringes of Society in her uncle's home, had heard about the statue garden. She still remembered one letter they had shared from a friend who had seen the work-in-progress.

A dozen commissioned statues of the favorite Greeks, a dozen more of historical figures, and all scattered about in beds of flowers meant to delight the senses.

And here she stood, with only a flight of stairs and a door between her and such magnificent beauty.

"Half an hour," she said aloud, then nodded firmly. She could spare that much. She would be outside and back in so quickly she would not even need a bonnet and gloves. She briefly looked down at her dress.

The deep blue gown she wore was cut for practicality, not fashion. The neck was high, the sleeves long, and there were no feminine ruffles or flounces, or any lace to speak of. But what did she care? It was not as though she was going to a garden party. She meant to take a hurried stroll, be seen by no one, and return to the schoolroom on the upper floor.

That decided, Alice went out the door and found the servants' staircase. When she accompanied the children, she was to keep to the main passages and stairs, but alone she could do as she pleased.

She passed a valet who gave her a quick bow and skirted by a maid who looked rather affronted at finding someone in her path. Then she was on the ground floor, and with just a few steps, she was out a door to the first terrace, which consisted of lawn furniture and tables meant for the household and guests to take their ease in the open air. Steps led down to the next level of gardens, and she took those quickly. After the first terrace where one could sit and enjoy the view, there were rose gardens, and then the slightly wilder gardens filled with riotous flowerbeds and columns of ivy; below that one she found the statues.

Her heart raced from her exertion, and Alice did not stop until she stood at the foot of the first statue she saw. "Who are you, then?" she asked the marble maiden. The woman stood holding a bowl in one hand and wheat in the other, looking out over the garden with a gentle expression.

Alice tapped her lip with one finger as she thought, before quietly whispering, "Hestia or Hera, a goddess of prosperity and harvest. Hm." She went on to the next, the statue of a man holding a bow and surrounded by purple and pink butter-cup-like flowers. "Anemones. Ah, that makes *you* Adonis." Alice smiled up at the Greek depiction of male beauty. Then she narrowed her eyes. He rather looked like the portrait of the duke she had passed on the grand staircase. "I wonder if the duke commissioned you, or if the sculptor sought to win his favor?" She giggled at herself and kept going.

Her time stolen from duty ran short. She needed to hurry, so as she went deeper into the gardens, she ran around the base of another statue to come to its front—and tripped over a pair of boots. Her momentum sent her sprawling face-first into the flowerbed.

Unladylike words trilled through her mind, learned when unsuspecting male relatives had let loose their caustic tongues within her hearing. But she clamped her lips against saying such things out loud, only to immediately taste dirt.

Alice tried to rise at the exact moment the owner of the other pair of legs attempted the same. Her foot slipped between a pair of ankles, tangling them both up. It also sent her face back into the flowers.

A rather masculine voice, likely belonging to those same legs, released a torrent of ill-tempered words. "What in blazes—if His Grace keeps allowing this, I will never complete my work."

What did the duke have to do with a man lying about in the gardens, where anyone might trip over him? She ought to offer an apology, but given his brusque reaction to the accident, he might not deserve one.

Alice groaned and settled for rolling over, instead. The first thing she saw was the top of the statue she had been attempting to view from the front. The figure was that of an imperious-looking woman, pointing almost directly at where Alice lay. She blinked.

A face appeared above her, alarmingly close. "You aren't one of the duke's daughters." He spoke almost gruffly, as though he disapproved of her anyway.

Thank heavens her spectacles remained in place. They allowed her to clearly make out every detail of the man kneeling at her side. He was a handsome fellow, despite the smudge of dirt across his cheek. He had black hair that fell across his forehead almost into his forest-filled eyes. His face was narrow, his lips wide, and a rather endearing little cleft marked the bottom of his chin.

All her female cousins from the tender age of fourteen to three and thirty would take notice of this man.

"Are you injured?" he asked, his black eyebrows pushing together. "Addled?"

Alice sucked in a breath. "I do not think so."

He nodded and extended a hand to her. He wore thick leather gloves, well-scratched and dirty. Alice took the offered hand, and with a swift movement he pulled her to her feet. While she was taller than Society considered fashionable, this man still had half a head on her in height.

"You ought to look where you are going." He abruptly turned away from her. The man released a long-suffering sigh. "It's gone. An absolute perfect specimen."

Narrowing her eyes, Alice glanced down where she had landed and crushed more than a few flowers. "There are many unhurt. Perhaps you might find another."

"Another. I suppose that will have to do." He sighed and stripped off his leather gloves, dropping them into an open wooden box filled with odd tools.

Though his accent was educated, not the same which she had caught sound of from the servants, his rough style of dress seemingly marked him as under the duke's employment. The box on the ground as someone who worked outdoors, with his hands. Botheration. Had she stumbled over a groundskeeper?

Alice twisted the ring around her right thumb with the fingers of the opposite hand. "Are there more beds of narcissus?"

"Hm?" His gaze left the ground to meet hers. "Narcissus?"

She gestured to the white and yellow flowers. "Are there more elsewhere in the castle's gardens?"

"Yes." He looked down at the flowers again, his shoulders slumping forward beneath his dirt-smudged coat. "I suppose finding more of that particular type of flora might lead me back to the *Pieris napi*. Though I cannot say I have seen those two coincide often."

Alice could identify many flowers by their common names, but his Latin immediately showed the state of her ignorance. Did gardeners usually refer to flowers in Latin? Perhaps he had a better education than most servants, which explained his lack of the local accent. Perhaps he was someone's younger son, who had found himself in need of employment beneath the status he had once enjoyed. She knew well enough that an adequate education might not lead to a favorable position in Society.

"I do apologize for disturbing you. I am afraid I was not paying attention in my hurry." A butterfly fluttered in the breeze, coming nearer the gentleman's shoulder.

He cocked one of those dark eyebrows at her. "A hurry? In a garden?" He finally seemed to give notice to her, his eyes sweeping up and down her frame in a cursory manner.

She reached up to tuck the hook of her spectacles more firmly behind one ear, sneakily ensuring her unruly curls had stayed in place during her fall. Though she wore no bonnet or gloves, Alice knew she appeared respectable enough.

"My name is Miss Sharpe. I'm the new governess to Her Grace's children. I thought to take in the gardens, but my time is short. I must return to the schoolroom." She gripped the side of her skirt, a sudden and dreadful thought coming to her. "I hope I did not venture out of bounds. No one said whether or not I could explore the gardens—" She cut herself off, recalling well enough how often her aunts had warned her against "prattling on and on."

The man tipped his head to one side at the same moment the little green and white butterfly—or was it a moth?—landed upon his shoulder. The effect was rather comical, given the situation, and Alice bit her bottom lip against a giggle.

"I cannot think why a member of the household, even a governess, would be barred from the gardens." His forehead wrinkled as he stared at her. "You have some dirt on your cheek. Just here." He tapped his own left cheek, beneath his eye.

A brief laugh tripped from her at last. "So do you, actually." She withdrew a handkerchief from her sleeve and wiped at her cheek, then held the cloth out to him. He stared at the linen, edged in embroidered rosebuds, as though surprised by it. Then he smiled and shook his head. It was a charming smile, a little crooked on one side.

"I'll have more than a bit of soil on my cheek by the end of the day. But thank you, Miss Sharpe."

She tucked the handkerchief away, then cut a glance at the

butterfly, now resting with open wings.

"Um." She took a quick step to the side. "You have a bit more than dirt on your shoulder, too, sir. There is a butterfly—I should not like it to be hurt. May I remove it?" A silly thing to ask, really. But what if he brushed it off and damaged the poor creature?

He stilled, as though her words had turned him into stone— every bit as much of a statue as the Aphrodite who stood above them while they spoke. *It has to be Aphrodite, really, given that she is pointing at a bed of Narcissus.* Greek myths had captivated Alice during her years of ducking into libraries to avoid the severe criticisms of relatives.

He spoke through barely parted lips, obviously trying to move as little as possible. "Is it white and green?"

Alice blinked up at him. "Yes?" What difference did the color make? And he acted as though she had told him he had a wasp waiting to sting him.

"I have forceps in that box." He pointed with a finger, not even raising his hand. "They have little nets on either side. Do you think...that is, would you mind using them to capture the butterfly?"

"Netted forceps?" Alice looked down again at the box, then up at the man. "I could use my hands. I will be gentle."

"No. Humans secrete oils and minerals which would be harmful to the wings. The forceps would be best, please."

Having never had anyone mention secretions of any kind to her, Alice hesitated while she wondered if she ought to take offense. He had said *humans.* And it sounded as though his last wish was to hurt the delicate creature. She bent down and reached for the box, pulling it closer to her. If he was trying to minimize his movements, she ought to do the same.

There were many odd things in the box, including small crates lined with netted fabric. But the forceps were easily found. She took them in hand, opened them, and stood slowly. The gardener hadn't moved at all. Neither had the butterfly.

Alice positioned the netted forceps carefully, then closed them gently over the little creature. It raised its wings as she moved, which seemed to be better for it. Alice brought the little net closer, peering at the butterfly and biting her lip.

"I do hope we haven't hurt it."

The antennae continued to move, as did the little legs. Alice let out the breath she had held the moment she captured the creature, rocking back on her heels. She had not crushed it. She raised her gaze to the man in front of her, unable to hold back her grin. "I caught it."

RUPERT RARELY INTERACTED WITH THE FAIRER MEMBERS OF his species for a reason. He had seen more than one Society miss latch onto a gentleman the way a female *Mantis religiosa* latched onto her mate before eating him. Not that a gentlewoman would *literally* eat him. But the figurative devouring of his life, his person, his time, and his funds, kept him from fully trusting the women who sent flirtatious smiles his way.

Miss Sharpe's smile was not at all coy, nor was it calculating. There was only true joy and surprise in her eyes and the curve of her lips. Indeed, her smile grew wide enough that he caught a flash of her teeth—something most women of his acquaintance would rather die than expose for fear of being perceived as vulgar.

When Miss Sharpe grinned, holding the netted forceps in a gentle grasp, he only saw beauty.

Blinking away that thought, Rupert rushed instead to find an empty insect cage for the butterfly, *Pieris napi*. "The green-veined white." He slid open the wooden door to the cage. "Would you release it in here, please, and then withdraw the forceps quickly?"

Her smile faded, but her nod was firm. He held the box in both hands, and she stepped nearer in order to peer into it before releasing the winged insect. He slid the door shut, then held the box up so they both could peer through the netting as the butterfly opened and closed its wings inside.

"How lovely." The whispered words brought his focus away from the white and green wings, settling it instead on the woman no more than a foot away from him. "What a magnificent way to study butterflies."

"And other insects." He stood to his full height, noting absently that she was rather tall for a woman. "Thank you for your help. I thought it had escaped."

Her bright blue eyes narrowed. They were rather an interesting color. What did they remind him of?

"Are you going to pin it to a box somewhere?" she asked, sounding terribly disapproving.

"I should not have the need to do so, this time. I prefer to study creatures while they're in movement. But I do have a rather extensive collection of insects."

Her nose wrinkled in a familiar expression of disgust. "Boxes of dead things." She shuddered. "What is the point of that?"

Rupert tucked the butterfly's box back into his crate. He had heard this opinion from any number of people before. He released a sigh. "It is for science, Miss Sharpe."

"Science?" She took a step back, tugging at the end of one sleeve. "I understand the initial study, but why *keep* them after they are no longer useful?"

He looked up at her from where he crouched, considering the question. "Because they are always useful. What if I find a new species? How would I know without comparing it to what I already know to be cataloged? Or, perhaps, I come upon a stronger magnification method. I could make greater inspection of a creature already in my collection, rather than finding a new one."

"I suppose a non-living insect would be easier to study through a microscope." The way she spoke, as though conceding the argument, made him study her more closely. "Have you a microscope? How extraordinary. I thought to ask for one, for the schoolroom. I did not see one this morning amid the shelves."

Before he could answer, she fixed him with a sudden wide-eyed expression. "Oh. I've been out too long. I must go. Do forgive me for rushing away. It was a pleasure to have met you." She dropped the slightest dip of a curtsy and darted away. She ran behind the statue looming over them, and when he leaned backward enough to follow her progress through the hedges, he saw she was moving with great speed back to the castle.

Rupert considered her fleeing form long after she had disappeared. Though dressed in dark clothing, she had bright, lively eyes that hinted at intelligence and good humor. She was young for a governess. Pretty, too.

The duke's three youngest children needed a firm hand. Given Miss Sharpe's worry over harming a delicate butterfly, he doubted she had one. And yet. When she had challenged his habit of keeping insects in boxes, her jaw tight and eyes full of censure, she had appeared rather severe.

Not that it mattered to him. The governess was none of his concern. He had promised the duke to catalog insects and plants alike, and that daunting task required his full attention.

He rubbed at his cheek and felt the dirt flake away. His valet would certainly tut over Rupert that evening, before dinner. There were guests coming, too, though Rupert could not remember who they were. That meant sitting at a table and trying to make conversation on topics other than his studies.

Rupert glanced at the disheveled flowerbed and chuckled. It was really too bad the governess would not be there. He had not even introduced himself.

Not that it mattered. A governess would stay in her schoolroom, apart from the family and servants alike. Which meant he would likely see no more of her quick smile.

What a shame.

CHAPTER 4

The schoolroom's disorder would *not* endear Alice to her employers.

When she stepped inside the door to survey the damage of her first day in her position, her heart sank. "Oh, dear. Perhaps we should have tidied up before dinner."

A book had been left open on the floor, pages spread like a bird had crashed mid-flight. Ink blots upon paper scattered across the round table reminded Alice of insects on flower petals.

No one had told her how much they expected her to tidy up and what she could leave for a maid.

The children ate their dinner with her in a small room near the kitchen, as would be the custom unless their father invited them to the formal dining table. Then they disappeared for their baths and beds.

She alone stood in the schoolroom.

Picking up the book, Alice saw from its title it had to belong to Lady Rosalind. At twelve, the girl should have known better than to leave it out like that.

The children and Alice had spent the afternoon looking through the schoolbooks to find topics that interested the children.

If Alice could build an educational schedule around things that made Lady Isabelle, Lady Rosalind, and Lord James curious, she would have a better time at keeping their attention.

The idea had struck her when she thought about the gardener, and how interested he seemed in insects. If a gardener could study the creeping things of the earth as well as flowers, why shouldn't children learn of things that mattered to them in addition to the work everyone expected them to do?

She needed to put some books aside for her own study and make lists of what they had discussed to see if the duke's library had more books they might use.

"Miss Sharpe? Are you in here?" When a maid came into the room in a rush, Alice looked up from the table, over a stack of books nearly as tall as she was when sitting down.

"Here I am!" She waved her hand in the air above the books. "Is anything wrong?"

"Wrong?" The maid spluttered. "Miss Sharpe, Her Grace sent for you to join them at dinner this evening. One of her guests is ill, and now the table is all put-out and uneven."

Alice froze, mid-way out of her seat. "Dinner with His Grace and their guests? You must be mistaken. Even if the numbers are wrong, they cannot want a governess."

"They do, Miss Sharpe." The maid gestured to the door. "Hurry. I'm to send you down straight away, but it took me too long to find you."

"But—but—" Alice's hands went up to her hair, then she touched her skirt. "I am not *dressed* for dinner."

"Then *get* dressed. Hurry." The maid came forward, took Alice by the arm, and pulled until Alice started walking. "You must hurry. There's no time for frippery. You're just an extra body at the table. Nearly everyone else is titled."

Alice knew well enough that the maid spoke the truth. Her presence would be ignored, most likely. They meant her to keep numbers even, the way some might put a block beneath a table leg to keep it from tilting too much to one side.

With the maid's help, Alice was out of her midnight blue dress and into one of the few evening gowns her great-aunt had told her to pack. There would be times when she must be present, if the children were invited to important events or performed in musical entertainment, and she had to dress properly for that.

"But never can you compete with a guest in your finery," her great-aunt had warned, casting all of Alice's favorite gowns into a trunk bound for the attic. She had left Alice only two evening gowns. One was the color of a crushed and wilted lilac, a shade Alice found rather mournful, and the other was a pale pink that did nothing for her complexion.

Alice wore the wilted-lilac that evening. It made her appear rather without color. They hardly touched her hair, except to loosen a few strands from the unfashionable bun. She kept on her spectacles and her father's ring, sliding gloves on to wear down to the table.

With no other adornments, Alice practically ran down the corridors to the main floor. She arrived in the corridor outside the dining room, where a footman waited for her.

He bowed when she approached. "Miss Sharpe. The guests are about to leave the drawing room to enter the dining room. You must wait here until all the guests have walked by, then you join the last gentleman at the rear of the party."

"Thank you." Alice gifted him what she hoped would appear as a confident smile. On the inside, her nerves started to twist, and her stomach clenched around the dinner she had already eaten with the children.

Eating at a table full of ladies and lords did not exactly intimidate her. She had grown up a member of the gentry, taking her meals at the dining tables of her relatives. Her family had expected Alice to make herself interesting enough to entertain their guests, without being too forward as to draw attention to herself. But the idea of sitting at the table of an employer, someone not expected to keep her on if she made a mistake, struck her differently.

Be personable, affable, but never so interesting as to attract comment on your behavior or person. The second wife of one of her uncles had given Alice that admonishment.

She smoothed a small wrinkle on her gown, then let her eyes roam up to the tall ceiling of the main corridor. Though the castle had only completed construction ten years previous, it had the air of a medieval fortress. The duke and duchess were avid collectors of antiques and artwork. Along the particular passage, they had hung shields along the top of the wall. Tapestries depicting ancient forests hung on the walls beneath those shields, and between every tapestry was an oil painting of either a landscape or a scene from British history.

The ducal couple had modeled the corridor, with its gray and white marble floors, in a style to impress upon the duke's guests of the might of England.

Liveried footmen opened a set of double doors on one side of the passage. Light and laughter spilled out just before the duchess and a male guest stepped out, followed by the duke and a female guest.

Two new footmen appeared out of doors nearer to where Alice stood, hidden in shadow now that light streamed in from other directions. The party made their way toward Alice and turned into the dining hall.

Alice waited with her eyes lowered, watching only the feet of each couple as they passed her. Fourteen couples went by before a lone pair of polished shoes appeared and then hesitated before her.

Alice stepped forward with a footman prepared to make introductions.

The footman sounded as formal as a majordomo or master of ceremonies, despite his quiet tone. "Mr. Gardiner, may I present

Miss Sharpe, the family governess and your dinner companion for the evening."

Alice curtsied, then raised her gaze at last to the poor gentleman stuck with a governess for the evening. She knew well enough that he would not be enthusiastic about the idea.

Except.

Black hair swept somewhat untidily across his brow, and peeking through the tips of his hair, glittering green eyes took her in. The gardener from that afternoon, sans dirt smudges and in a forest green coat of superfine, was not a servant.

He was a guest.

"Miss Sharpe. A pleasure." He bowed, then extended his hand to her.

Gulping back a squeak of surprise, Alice allowed him to take her hand and place it upon his sleeve. "Mr. Gardiner."

Their exchange took only seconds, putting them barely behind the last couple to enter the dining room. Mr. Gardiner kept his head better than Alice did, thankfully, as he took her directly to a chair in the middle of the table, to the duchess's right. He held her chair out for her. Alice sank into it most gratefully.

Then Mr. Gardiner sat next to her, appearing perfectly at ease by the surprise meeting. Of course, he could not be nearly so surprised as she. The man she had taken for some sort of servant, a groundskeeper, was a gentleman. An important enough gentleman to sit at a duke's table, amid other members of nobility.

Alice's mortification grew, extending beyond previous bounds, as she admitted to herself that she had hoped to meet the man again.

But not like this.

She glanced at him from the corner of his eye. He smiled. She blinked and hastily turned away.

The pale, silent woman eating at Rupert's left might bear a physical resemblance to the governess he met earlier, but her manners had undergone a severe change. The Miss Sharpe he met in the garden had brimmed with energy, her countenance naturally bright and intelligent. But now she sat stiffly, her gaze unfocused behind the glass of her spectacles.

The informality of their garden meeting verged on comical. When the butler informed him in apologetic tones that the governess would be his dinner companion, Rupert had perked up somewhat. He had been slated to keep company with the local vicar's wife, a woman full of nervous laughter and incapable of speaking on subjects outside of her personal charity work. With the vicar's wife fallen ill, and her husband still in attendance, he accepted the reprieve gladly.

Perhaps the duke's guests intimidated her. As her assigned escort and dinner companion, it fell to Rupert to set her at ease. "Miss Sharpe?"

Her blue eyes widened a fraction before meeting his. "Yes, Mr. Gardiner?"

Rupert leaned toward her to murmur. "I am glad to see you again. It gives me the opportunity to inform you that I released the little butterfly you caught. Back into the wilds of Clairvoir."

After a quick glance at others sitting around the table, Miss Sharpe spoke in a soft tone unlikely to carry farther than his ears. "I am pleased to learn it, sir. I imagine she is grateful she was only your captive for a short time."

Rupert tipped his head to the side. "You think butterflies have the capacity for gratitude?"

She lifted one shoulder less than an inch, toying with the slice of candied beet on her plate. "I cannot be certain they do. Can you be certain they do not?"

"Most of the world would say it is not possible for so tiny a creature to have thoughts or feelings." Rupert tapped his fingers on the arm of his chair, then reached for his cup.

"Most think creatures of insignificance, unworthy of notice by their betters, are therefore unworthy of everything." She dropped her hand into her lap. "Simply because we do not know the inner-workings of an animal or insect, and cannot know, does not make them beneath our care."

Rupert lowered his cup without drinking, studying instead her profile. No hint of a smile or laughter took away from her words. "Do you care about butterflies in general, Miss Sharpe?"

"Yes. I think most should. Do they not carry pollen from one flower to another, as bees do? For creatures performing such an important function, they merit some thought." Miss Sharpe's smile appeared, albeit briefly. "I might ask if *you* care about butterflies, sir, given your collection of them."

"I do. Of course." Ah. Now her strange behavior grew under-standable. He had thought that someone might have told her about him, given his position as a guest of the duke. But she had only taken up her position the day before. Perhaps it was arrogant of him to assume people spoke about his work when he was not present. Certainly, not everyone found the subject of his studies worth notice. "I am an amateur entomologist and botanist."

Miss Sharpe's smile changed into a puzzled frown. "I am sorry. Entomologist?"

"A relatively new term for my branch of study." He took a turn glancing about, to be certain no one else listened. "Some call it insectology. I am a naturalist who studies insects." The young ladies of his acquaintance did not consider the mention of insects appropriate dinner table conversation.

"Oh." Apparently, given the way Miss Sharpe's blue eyes brightened, she was not like most people in that regard. "*That* was what you were doing. This whole afternoon, I thought you were in the gardens inspecting the flowers. Then I thought your enthu-siasm over the butterfly was something of a hobby."

He injected his words with some humor rather than take offense. "I suppose some would call it that."

Most of his acquaintances in the world of science termed his interest in bugs a hobby. Some added the adjective *disgusting* to qualify their opinion on the fact. Except for his father, whose studies centered on birds. Ornithology commanded a great deal more respect than the newly renamed study of insects. But Rupert's father had always encouraged him to follow his passion.

"I have so many questions." Miss Sharpe's voice raised just slightly, to a normal conversation level. "Are you a member of the Linnean Society? I have a cousin who dabbles in botany. He subscribes to their journal, and I have read some of the articles. I confess to finding the most interest in things which pertained to flowers." Ah, there was that spark in her eyes.

Rupert sat back a little in his chair. "You? A lady, reading scientific journals?"

The spark fizzled and turned dark and smoky instead. "Yes, as fantastic as it might seem, I—a woman—have a curiosity about the natural world." She turned to give more attention to her plate, angling herself in such a way as to avoid looking at him.

Her tone held enough of a chill in it to make him shiver. Apparently, he was the one now in danger of giving offense. "Miss Sharpe. I meant—"

"Pardon me, Mr. Gardiner." The baroness to his right, Lady Alterby, attempted to gain his attention.

Rupert wanted to sink into his chair. First he insulted an intelligent woman, now he had been brought to realize he had neglected his other dinner companion. He fixed a smile in place and turned to speak to the elderly woman. "Yes, my lady?"

"I have just learned that your uncle is a solicitor in Peterborough. I have a nephew there. Perhaps they are acquainted. But I had thought to ask you if you have been there of late. I have not gone in years..." Lady Alterby kept speaking, her cadence more like the drone of a common housefly than the spritely way Miss Sharpe had conversed with him.

Though he attempted to enter an actual conversation with

Lady Alterby, it became apparent that she had more of a desire to reminisce about her time in Peterborough than exchange thoughts or opinions on any subject.

Finally, she turned to the dinner guest at her other side, the vicar, and nettled him about where he had taken orders.

Rupert took the reprieve gratefully. "Miss Sharpe? Would you like some of the"—he peered at the platter in confusion a moment —"braised carrots and rabbit?"

She had remained quiet since their exchange, no one else engaging her. But she nodded tightly in response to his question.

Rupert did his duty, serving her from the new platter a footman placed upon the table, but she seemed as inclined to push that portion of the meal as she had the last.

"Miss Sharpe?"

"Yes, Mr. Gardiner?" She did not turn to look at him. The lavender gown she wore made her appear quite pale. Or perhaps his company displeased her.

"Are you unwell?" he asked, lowering his voice and leaning closer to her.

He did not miss the way her hand tightened around her fork the instant before she looked at him. "I am perfectly well. Thank you."

Rupert stumbled over his thoughts. "I am sorry. I only thought —since you are not eating—" He cut himself off and took a drink to stave off any more of his own foolishness.

She sent him a perplexed glance, stabbed at a slice of purple potato, and put the whole thing in her mouth at once. Then she raised her eyebrows, daring him to make another comment. Instead he laughed, but as he was still sipping at his drink, he gulped the wine, so it went entirely the wrong direction down his throat.

Rupert choked, put a napkin over his mouth and coughed, but a burning sensation remained. His eyes started to water, and everyone at the table fell silent.

Someone pressed a cup into his hand, and he drank, but that proved a mistake, too.

When he finally had control of his lungs and throat, eyes streaming, he looked up. Everyone stared at him. Except for Miss Sharpe, who had somehow managed to shrink despite sitting with proper posture.

With heat running up the back of his neck and into his ears, he placed a hand over his heart and gave the semblance of a bow from his seat. "I beg your pardon, Your Graces. Do forgive me."

"Are you quite all right, Gardiner?" the duke asked from his end of the table.

"Yes, Your Grace." Rupert stood and bowed properly. "Merely a difficult swallow, sir." His humiliation mounted.

"Very well. Do eat more carefully, sir." The duke's light tone gave others the leave to laugh and go back to their conversations.

Rupert lowered himself back into his chair, took one small sip of his wine, then turned his full attention to the woman on his left. "Miss Sharpe."

She was attempting to pretend there was a wall between them, given her refusal to look at him. Had his accident somehow embarrassed her?

He leaned closer to her and lowered his voice. "Miss Sharpe?"

She hesitantly turned to him, then whispered, "I am sorry I made you cough."

Rupert's heart softened further toward her. "I owe you an apology, too. I did not mean to give you insult before. About the scientific journal."

Those blue eyes were wide and apologetic behind her spectacles. "You did not? I mean—of course not." She dropped her gaze to her lap where he saw she twisted a ring around her thumb. "It must surprise you, though. My cousin always thought it odd for a woman to show interest—"

"For anyone, Miss Sharpe." He forced a smile. He had already humiliated himself that evening. Making a clear, thorough apology would not hurt his pride. "I can count on one hand the number of acquaintances I have, outside of the naturalists I've befriended, who have even looked at a journal published by the Linnean or the Royal Society. It is unique, no matter your sex."

The color reappeared in her cheeks. "I see." She opened her mouth, ready to say more, but the baroness called for Rupert's attention again. He spared Miss Sharpe an apologetic smile, then gave his other dinner companion the courtesy of listening to what she had to say.

Rupert's coughing fit had drawn too much attention for anyone to ignore him from that point forward. Regrettably, he could not turn again for a private word with the pretty governess. Miss Sharpe kept her head down and her concentration on her plate until dinner ended, when she slipped away at the same moment the servants cleared the last dish.

Disappointment settled upon Rupert's shoulders, heavy enough to keep him from enjoying the rest of the evening. He had wanted to find out why the governess's eyes lit up at the mention of scientific journals. He wanted to know what she thought of the flowers present in the duke's gardens.

He wanted to know more about *her*.

CHAPTER 5

Alice berated herself all morning long. Silently.

The moment dinner had finished the evening before, Alice had slipped away without a word to anyone. She had filled her role, balancing the table, and she wanted nothing more than to escape without any further notice.

The children went through their lessons on literature, penmanship, and French with ease. They were advanced in those areas. Then she settled Lord James with supplies to draw out a map of his father's estate, while she gave the girls samplers to practice their embroidery.

Pretending to read a book, Alice sat in a chair where she could easily watch them all. The duke would send Lord James to school in January, as befitting a future duke, but she would keep the girls until their mother deemed it time for them to leave the schoolroom as their eldest sister had.

Alice had only caught glimpses of Lady Josephine, who was nineteen years of age. She had sat near her mother at dinner the evening before, between two handsome men at least a decade older than she.

Lady Josephine had captivated and charmed her companions

throughout dinner. She had a beauty that many Englishwomen would long for, with deep brown hair and eyes, and a petite form that spoke of grace and good breeding. It was interesting, the differences between the duke's eldest daughter and Alice. Lady Josephine was younger but had more influence and command of a room than Alice would ever experience.

Not that Alice envied her that. In all her time learning how to disappear until someone wanted her, Alice did not think she would enjoy having people constantly on the watch for what she would say or do.

She had not even managed to hold the attention of one gentleman, nor to converse without taking offense. The memory of that horrid scene made her groan aloud.

"Is something the matter, Miss Sharpe?" Lady Isabelle, the eldest of the children in the schoolroom, sounded concerned. "Are you ill?"

Alice peered over the edge of her book, keeping her expression neutral. "I am perfectly well, thank you. I merely read something disturbing." She turned a page in the book. "Continue your work."

Lady Isabelle exchanged a glance with her sister, who huffed. Perhaps the two had hoped an ill governess meant a cessation of their work.

Lady Rosalind stabbed her embroidery needle rather harshly into the fabric. "I wish there was more to do than school. Mother and Father's guests all leave today, and that was the only interesting thing about this week."

"That and meeting our new governess," Lady Isabelle corrected with haste. The girl would make a politician a wonderful wife someday. "But at least they are not all going."

The younger sister paused in her work to glare across the table at Lady Isabelle. "You *cannot* mean to be glad about Mr. Gardiner. He might look young, but he's as grumpy as an admiral."

Although curious how many admirals the child had met, Alice

remained silent. She listened instead. Why would the gentleman remain behind when the other members of the visiting party dispersed?

Shrugging in an almost French manner, Lady Isabelle answered without lifting her gaze from her work. "I do like looking at him, though. He can be kind, too. But I dislike when he speaks of his horrid little insects." She shivered dramatically.

Lord James paused in his map-making to glower at both sisters. "He still won't let me use his nets or cages to catch spiders."

Lady Rosalind sniffed. "As well he should not. You would do something horrid with them."

Alice turned another page in her book, though she had not read a single line in some time.

"But Father commissioned Mr. Gardiner, so should he not do as we say?" Lord James asked, a near whine creeping into his tone.

As governess, it was time to speak up. "Your father also commissioned *me* to teach you until January, Lord James. But I do not do what you say."

The boy muttered, "Then what's the point of being a duke's son?"

Alice lowered her book to her lap. "Dear me. I hope you do not mean to be tyrannical with your powers. I would imagine the point of being a lord has less to do with telling others what to do and more with how to exert your influence in a way that betters the country and the people under your care."

Although the boy did not appear chastened, he furrowed his brow and went back to work on his map.

Mr. Gardiner had been commissioned by the Duke of Montfort to do something. Something regarding insects. Given his state the day before, capturing and observing the butterfly, whatever it was took his full attention.

How fortunate he was to have not only a subject which interested him, but which others found useful.

A knock at the door brought everyone's gaze up. Alice rose. "Enter, please." She put down the poor book she had used as a prop for her wool-gathering.

A woman Alice had not yet met entered the room, dressed in the clothing of a gentlewoman. "Do pardon me for interrupting, but Her Grace has sent for Lady Isabelle and Lady Rosalind." She was taller than Alice, with dark brown ringlets of hair styled in curls, and flashing eyes that bespoke a good sense of humor.

Both girls immediately came to their feet. Alice checked the clock on the schoolroom mantel. "I imagine you will move on to your art lessons after you attend your mother, so I will see you both at two o'clock unless informed otherwise."

"Yes, Miss Sharpe." The girls spoke and curtsied in unison, then left the room with barely concealed glee. Given the time of day, Alice would guess their mother had invited them to take refreshment with her. It was likely the first time since the guests had arrived the week before that they would have the opportunity to spend time with the duchess alone.

The woman at the door watched them walk away, then looked back into the room. "We have not been introduced yet, Miss Sharpe. I am Emma Arlen, companion to Lady Josephine since her entrance into Society last year." She came into the room, clasping her hands before her.

Alice relaxed. Here was someone in the household in a position similar to her own. Not a part of the family, but not truly part of the staff. "It is a pleasure to meet you, Miss Arlen. I believe this is the first time I have even caught a glimpse of you."

"The castle is quite large." Miss Arlen raised her eyebrows. "It is a wonder more of us do not get lost or marooned in the wrong wing, waiting for someone to rescue us."

That elicited a laugh from Alice. "I have done my best not to stray from the main halls for just that purpose."

"Wise of you. I understand you went to dinner last night. I

was sorry to miss you there. We might have enjoyed a pleasant conversation afterward."

"Oh, yes. I balanced the table when the vicar's wife fell ill." Alice immediately wondered why they had asked her, rather than the eldest daughter's companion, who ranked higher than Alice in the hierarchy of staff.

Miss Arlen tilted her head to the side, as though she had heard Alice's unspoken thought. "My family lives nearby, and it was my evening to be with them." She gestured to Alice with a graceful wave of her hand. "I should like to come to know you better, Miss Sharpe, now that we have met properly. Perhaps the two of us might take tea together tomorrow? Lady Josephine is to receive instruction from her grandmother, and I need not be present."

If Miss Arlen could be a friend, Alice's time at the castle would certainly be more enjoyable. "That would be wonderful. I take tea with the children."

Lord James huffed, making a dark mark on his map. "I dislike tea."

"La, sir. No Englishman ought to speak so." Miss Arlen ruffled his hair with familiarity. "What if I have cook send up your favorite biscuits? Do you think you would mind a tea party so much then?"

He squinted up at her. "Do you even know my favorite?"

Miss Arlen squinted back at the challenge. "Of course I do. The cinnamon biscuits made with molasses."

The boy feigned a deep sigh. "I suppose you can come to tea, then."

Miss Arlen and Alice both laughed. "Do not be too difficult for Miss Sharpe. Show her how charming you can be." Miss Arlen looked up at Alice again, her eyes bright. "I have known the family all my life. If any of the children give you trouble, tell me. I can offer up wonderful ideas on bribes or torture, whichever you prefer."

"Let us hope the torture is unnecessary." Alice narrowed her eyes at the boy but did not hide her smile. "I look forward to our tea tomorrow. I have the feeling it will be most informative as well as enjoyable."

"Very." Miss Arlen curtsied. "Until tomorrow." When she closed the door behind her, leaving only Lord James and Alice in the room, Alice came closer to the table to examine the boy's map. He had made substantial progress since starting that morning.

It seemed a shame to keep him cooped up in the schoolroom when his sisters were away doing something else.

"Would you like to go play in the garden, my lord?" Alice asked. He immediately dropped his pencil and looked up at her, eyes hopeful. "I think you could use some fresh air before you go to your art lesson."

"Yes, please." He pushed away from the table. "Can we go right now?"

Alice laughed. "Let me get my parasol and a few other things, then we can enjoy the sunshine."

"I'll get my skipping rope and chalk." The boy vanished out of the schoolroom, calling over his shoulder. "I'll meet you in the hall, Miss Sharpe."

It only took Alice a few moments to gather bonnet, gloves, parasol, and her sketchbook. After wandering about unprepared the day before, she had placed her things at the ready for another garden adventure. When she arrived in the hall, she saw her young charge with arms full of his own entertainments.

"Have you seen the big lily fountain yet, Miss Sharpe?" he asked, leading the way down the corridor to the main staircase. "It's sunken into the ground, so it looks like a pond. There are even frogs living inside of it."

Although trusting the young boy when so near amphibians gave her misgivings, Alice responded cheerfully. "I have not seen more than a few of the statues. Is the lily fountain a favorite of yours?"

He started rattling off all the reasons he enjoyed that corner of the gardens. Most of them seemed to be related to the general wildness of the plant life there. "It almost looks like no one ever gardens there, but I know they do. Because the grass is always short, and the pavers never grown over. But plants are everywhere."

The fashion of allowing gardens to appear as wild as woodlands had not entirely gone out of style, and with someone like the countess promoting such a thing in her gardens, it was likely to be popular for some time yet.

Alice followed Lord James all the way outside, then down the terraced levels of the garden. A large willow tree was the first sign that they had entered a new section of cultivated land. They passed beneath it, the long delicate limbs parting as easily as curtains to allow them through. When they stepped out on the other side, Alice gasped.

The spot might well become *her* favorite, too.

The fountain was sunk beneath the ground, and the only way to recognize it was manmade rather than a pond was its near perfect circular shape. In the middle of the fountain was a gray stone statue of two swans, heads bent toward one another. In the water itself grew lily pads, tall rushes, and the brilliant purple-loosestrife. Alice had only encountered the tall, bright spikes of flowers once before, visiting a family member who lived near King's Lyn.

There were long grasses scattered about the area, but a cobbled walking path going around the fountain was perfectly maintained. There was a bench on the other side of the fountain, and a tall oak shading half of the area bore a swing, too.

"This is beautiful," she whispered, and immediately went to sit on the clover path near the flowers. Alice opened her sketchbook and turned over pages until she found one empty. She went to work immediately, capturing the gentle curve in the tall green stalk. A butterfly that looked rather like a leaf fluttered by, landing on one of the flowers.

Lord James busied himself with his chalk and the cobblestones. When she glanced over once, after he had been quiet for a time, she saw he was putting faces on individual stones. Some were quite hideous, others amusing. Alice hid her smile behind her sketch and went back to her own drawing.

Periodically, Alice checked the watch she wore. It had been a gift from the same great-aunt who found her the position of governess for the duke's children. Though the watch might have looked lovely on a chain or chatelaine, it was far more practical to keep it on a ribbon Alice could slip between the pages of a book or into a reticule.

A quarter of an hour remained until they must leave for Lord James to attend his art lesson when the willow branches stirred, and Mr. Gardiner came into view. He wore a broad-brimmed hat more suitable to a fisherman than a gentleman, had a large basket tucked under one arm, along with a long-poled-net, and in his other arm he had books and a small box.

His gaze were so fixed on the sunken fountain that he did not even notice Alice and the little boy right away.

It was Lord James that called his attention to them with a gleeful shout. "Mr. Gardiner! Are you catching dragonflies again today?"

Mr. Gardiner started, then focused on the little boy. His gaze rose to sweep the surrounding area, and he spotted Alice on the bench. For no accountable reason, save residual embarrassment from the night before, Alice's cheeks grew warm.

Too much sun, she told herself.

She rose from her place on the bench, gripping the sides of her sketchbook.

"Not dragonflies today." He came further in, then bent over to carefully deposit his armload of supplies on the clover near the fountain. "I am releasing some specimens, then drawing the flowers."

"Oh." The boy's interest immediately dissipated. He crouched lower to the ground and went back to his chalk drawing.

Mr. Gardiner directed his stare at Alice again. "Miss Sharpe, it is good to see you again."

She curtsied. "Mr. Gardiner. I hope you're well today."

"Perfectly." He approached her while wearing an amiable expression. "You left too quickly after dinner. I regretted your absence. I hope I did not drive you away."

Had he really missed her? Even if not, he showed more thoughtfulness than most of her acquaintances by saying so. "Of course not, Mr. Gardiner. My duties as governess require an early start, which in turn requires an early evening retirement." She did not have to say that governesses were generally unwanted creatures when it came to evening entertainments.

"That makes sense. I prefer to be up with the sun. Insects are far busier during the cooler hours. I imagine they dislike heat as much as the rest of us." His eyes sparkled at her, alluding to their conversation from the day before. He gestured to her sketchbook, still all politeness. "Are you drawing the fountain scene? It is a bit of genius work, is it not? The dowager duchess designed this garden, I believe."

Alice pulled her sketchbook a little closer. Would he think her foolish if he saw? Perhaps not, as he apparently spent hours and hours observing insects. "Not the garden in its entirety. Merely the flowers." There, they had both done enough to be considered polite by Society's standards. He would withdraw to his own business.

Except, if anything, he appeared more interested than before. "Your interest in flowers extends beyond glancing at their pictures in publications?"

A laugh escaped her lips, though it was somewhat rueful. "I believe most ladies sketch flowers from time to time, Mr. Gardiner. Society rather demands that we are schooled in sketching things that are reminders of feminine beauty."

"I suppose that is true, but I find most give up realistic depictions in favor of the more artistic." He sighed and scratched behind his ear, his gaze going back to the pond. His next inquiry was merely polite, instead of curious, which gave her leave to relax. "Which flower has captured your interest?"

Stretching the book out to him, Alice attempted to sound unruffled. "You may look if you like."

He came closer to accept the book and flipped open the soft red cover. Then he looked from the sketch of the purple-loosestrife to her, then the real thing, then back to her.

"It is anatomically correct." One of his dark eyebrows arched upward at the same moment his head tilted to the side. Without asking, he turned the page and spotted the last sketch she had done before coming to Clairvoir. She had taken the time to color it in with pastels.

"Oh, that is only a flower I found near King's Lyn. The cook there keeps a patch to make tea for my uncle's gout." Alice's voice trailed away, and she felt her cheeks burn. He didn't care about her uncle's gout, her drawings, or her. Yet something made her squeeze out the last of her explanation. "She calls it a *speedwell*."

"A *Veronica chamaedrys*," Mr. Gardiner murmured, though he nodded as though it were not a correction. With one finger, he traced the main flower before he looked at the detail of the leaves she had drawn along the side. She had attempted to recreate the illustrated plates in one of the Royal Society journals. In the scientific magazines, they always represented the plants in full, with more detailed sketches of their individual parts along the border of the page. "The germander speedwell. Londoners nearly eradicated it at the end of the last century, for that gouty tea. It has other purported properties, too. Real or imagined, I do not know."

Well then. Perhaps he *did* care. At least about the flower. As a man interested in entomology, she had not expected his knowledge of botany.

"Miss Sharpe. These are remarkable renderings of plants. Do

you enjoy drawing flora?" He gave her such a look as to make her hesitate in answering. Alice sensed it was not an idle question.

Though inclined to bite her lip and shrink away from answering, Alice answered quietly. "Yes. I do. Flowers fascinate me."

He handed her back her sketchbook. "One moment, please. If you would indulge me, I would like to show you something." He bolted away, going to the things he had dropped beside the manufactured pond. He shuffled through the pile and drew out a sketchbook not dissimilar to hers. The leather of his cover was green, she saw as he approached.

He undid the twist of leather meant to keep the covers closed and all loose-leaf paper inside. Opening the book, he held it against one arm while his free hand paged through the individual sheets. Then he pulled one out with a triumphant, "Ah-ha!"

Mr. Gardiner handed her the paper. "What do you think of this?"

She took the paper when he offered it and studied the drawing. She tipped the paper to one side to study the colors. The flower was yellow, but only one shade. The leaves about it were oblong, almost pointed on one end, and the stalk tall. But it took her a moment to identify the five-petaled flower. "Is it a primrose?"

"A common flower." He pointed to the insect he had drawn next to the flower, a fuzzy bee-fly that appeared so realistic, Alice nearly touched the page to feel the soft tufts on its body. The wings were iridescent, allowing her to see, through them, the shape of the insect's body. "And a common insect, terribly misunderstood by many gardeners. I have found the bee-fly to be a regular visitor to the primroses. I have chosen to depict them together. But you see that while I have devoted a great deal of attention to the detail of the bee-fly, the flower has been... Hm."

"Neglected," she supplied. "Yes, I see that." But why, when he was obviously a skilled artist?

As though he had heard her question, Mr. Gardiner tapped

the flower on the page. "Flowers are essential to many insects. They survive on the pollen and nectar, the petals and leaves, they make homes among the roots. And His Grace has commissioned me to compile a scientific catalog of flowers and insects here in the Clairvoir gardens. It is a complicated undertaking, and I find I prefer spending my time on the insects."

He grimaced when she glanced up at him. "That will never do, of course. I must properly display both. I only have until the end of August to finish the work, and there are thousands of insects. Hundreds of plants."

The enormity of the undertaking made Alice's shoulders slump, but at the same time she admired Mr. Gardiner. "There is a vast deal for you to accomplish, sir, in a short time."

"Indeed. I wonder, perhaps, if you might be interested in helping me." When Alice's gaze jerked back to him, he leaned closer to her, speaking quickly. "I do not dare suggest you take on my responsibilities, Miss Sharpe. That would be highly dishonest. But if you could assist me, when your time permits, as a colorist or to help me fill in details, I would be eternally grateful. I will not insult you by offering funds for such work, but I would credit you freely in the finished report and any subsequent publications."

Alice's lips parted and her mouth went dry. Did he mean to suggest that her name would appear in a scientific document? In the report he prepared for the duke, one of the most powerful men in England? Or perhaps, she thought, with a strange burning in her stomach, in a public journal or magazine.

With her heart racing, Alice pressed the paper into his chest. Then she fairly jumped backward when his hand came up to catch the sketch, covering hers quite by accident. She had removed her gloves to draw, and he wore none. The momentary warmth transferred from his palm to the back of her hand seemed to travel up her arm and into her chest.

"I—I have duties enough, Mr. Gardiner. Though I thank you for your generous offer." Alice took another step backward.

He could not know—How could he?—that she had dreamed of such a thing. Dreamed of being a person of notice, if only for a moment or two. Her name, her drawings, under the eye of anyone of importance gave her a thrill of excitement.

But bringing such attention to herself would embarrass her family. She was certain of it. They never wanted her to be seen as anything other than part of the furnishings of their houses. She was beneath the notice of anyone of importance.

And what would the duke say, if he discovered his governess spent any amount of time doing something other than what he paid her to do? She shivered and wrapped both arms around her sketchbook, taking another step back.

Mr. Gardiner frowned at her, though not in a disapproving way. He appeared confused. "If I have offended you again, Miss Sharpe, please forgive me. I did not mean to upset you."

With an abrupt shake of her head she tried to reassure him. "I am not offended." But she turned away from him to call to her charge. "Lord James, it is time to go inside for your art lesson." She curtsied to Mr. Gardiner without looking. "Good afternoon, sir. It was pleasant to see you again."

Then she fled, in as dignified a manner as possible.

Lord James scrambled after her, and when they were on the other side of the willow tree he shouted, "Slow down, Miss Sharpe."

Chastened, Alice waited for him to draw even with her. Mr. Gardiner was not in pursuit, after all. She needn't outrun him, or his request for assistance.

Alice bit the inside of her cheek, holding her sketchbook tighter.

Here someone had finally taken more than a moment's interest in her, in something she could do, and she had fled like a rabbit beneath a hawk's shadow.

CHAPTER 6

Chin in hand, Rupert studied the somewhat fumbling movements of a *Carabus violaceus* in one of the small wooden cages upon his desk. The bright violet coloring of the beetle put him in mind of the dress Miss Sharpe had worn to dinner two nights previously. Not that he would ever admit such a thing aloud. Even he knew that women did not enjoy being compared to insects. No matter that *he* thought it a compliment.

"Billings?"

His valet, on the other side of the room tidying Rupert's shaving things, answered. "Yes, sir?"

"Do you believe women to have inferior intelligence?" He turned to see his valet's reaction to the question.

Billings raised both eyebrows but did not even look up from arranging the soap and brushes needed for Rupert's evening shave. "I have a mother and five sisters, Mr. Gardiner. Not only would they box my ears if I said yes, but they could give any number of arguments and examples to demonstrate the opposite."

With a chuckle, Rupert leaned back against the corner of the desk. "My father has said women are less intelligent. He has never made the mistake of saying so in front of my mother, come to think of it." Rupert considered for a moment, then sighed. "There is a Swiss entomologist who specializes in bees. He is completely blind. But he carries out all his work with the help of his wife. She acts as secretary, or so people say. But I have to wonder if she could do so much, assist him in publishing all his findings and cataloging all his research, without being as intelligent as he."

"What of the botanist you met in London last year at your club? Mr. Banks, wasn't it?" Billings brought a chair from along the wall and moved it before the mirror. "You said he claimed to have been influenced by his sister."

"Miss Sarah Banks. Yes. She edited the manuscript he published about his voyage to Newfoundland." Rupert scrubbed his hands through his hair and immediately intercepted a disapproving glare from Billings. He grinned sheepishly.

"Sir, please leave your hair, facial and that atop your head, to me." Billings gestured to the chair. "If you are ready, all is prepared."

Settling into the chair, Rupert continued the conversation. "My point, Billings, is that if women have intelligence equal to men, as several women of note have proven, why are they denied entrance into so many of our societies?"

Billings put a white cloth around Rupert's neck, then lifted the soap pot to create lather with a brush. "It is not my place to say, sir."

Rupert grunted in dissatisfaction. He remained silent throughout Billings's ministrations, his thoughts again on Miss Sharpe. Her intelligent eyes, quick wit, and talent with her pencils marked her as a lady he should wish to know.

Why had she withdrawn with such rapidity, and apparent horror, when he suggested her help with his project?

Perhaps, like Billings, she did not think it her place. Though she had been born a gentlewoman, made most obvious by her education and mannerisms, she supported herself through employment. Though she claimed to take no offense, she had left far too quickly for any other explanation.

The situation disturbed him enough that Rupert had mentally rehearsed the scene from the day before more times than he could count. Governess the woman might be, but he needed an answer to the situation. Perhaps he could seek her out again. She had not come to dinner the evening before, as he expected given her status, and would not be present that evening.

A word alone with Miss Sharpe would clear up the situation. But a word alone with an unwed woman in the duke's employment might also lead to trouble.

The valet finished the shave and styled Rupert's hair swiftly, then his hand lingered on a pair of silver sheers. "Sir, might I suggest a haircut?"

The fringe falling across Rupert's forehead bothered the valet more than it did the master. Rupert shook his head and pulled off the cloth protecting his clothing. "Not today." He scrutinized first his appearance and then his valet in the mirror.

"Billings, do you think you could discover something for me without raising suspicion from the staff? I should like to know the schedule of a female member of the household, without causing any injury to reputation."

Billings reacted as though Rupert had asked the man to arrange an assignation. His jaw went slack, and his eyes bulged. "A woman's schedule? Sir, in all our years together, you've never asked such a thing." Then the valet narrowed his eyes. "It is not my place to ask why." But that was exactly what Billings did.

Rupert had to laugh at the dramatic reaction, and he tried to ignore the heat rising beneath his collar. "Not for any reprehensible reason, Billings. On my honor, I have no intention of behaving poorly. That is my point in asking if it can be done without injury. I merely wish to discover a time when I might have a word with a lady without anyone arriving to the wrong conclusion when we speak together."

"I can make inquiries." Billings stiffened. "Who is the lady in question?"

"Miss Sharpe. The governess."

"The governess." Billings relaxed. "I suppose you might speak with her anywhere except behind a closed door, sir. No one will much care or notice otherwise."

The statement brought Rupert to a pause, midway to standing. "But she is the daughter of a gentleman, and in the duke's household."

Billings's expression shifted from relaxed to the more formal mask of a servant. "As you say, sir. I believe an open door will be sufficient in this circumstance."

Rupert's thoughts shifted to Miss Sharpe's interaction with him that morning. Standing as close as he had to examine first her sketches and then his own, he had seen in her eyes an emotion he rarely encountered when he spoke of science, of insects, of botany. It went beyond polite interest. She had been as thrilled with the subjects under discussion as he, despite her reluctance to share her drawings.

A meeting of the minds had nearly occurred. Rupert knew it. But he had bungled things, somehow. Perhaps if he fixed them, if he only explained to Miss Sharpe, he would see that glimmer again.

CHAPTER 7

Morning lessons included penmanship, French, mathematics for Lord James, and reviewing household accounting books for the young ladies. The general subjects kept Alice on her toes, walking from one of her students to the others, while all three sat around a table in the schoolroom.

Their mother, an amateur architect, had also assigned the children to study Greek designs. None of the three shared their mother's passion. In fact, when Alice had suggested they each pick a topic of study that appealed to them, their choices had quite surprised her.

Lady Isabelle had asked about the study of religion, a curious subject for a girl of fourteen. Lady Rosalind showed an interest in studying the Dutch masters, as her family possessed two Van Dyke paintings. That left Lord James to claim he wanted to build a functioning, miniature catapult. For the sake of sounding more academic than not, Alice termed his studies *historical engineering*.

After they accomplished studying the general subjects, and before tea, Alice settled in her favorite chair while the children sat at a table near her. They were each absorbed in books regarding their subject, with even Lord James reading about medieval sieges in an English history book.

A quarter of an hour passed before the knock on the door disturbed the silence. Alice checked her watch. Miss Arlen had arrived early.

She rose and went to the door to speak with the lady's companion, to beg of her to return in half an hour, but when she peeped out of the doorway her eyes met a cleft chin.

As Alice lifted her gaze upward, a flush of heat seared her cheeks. "Mr. Gardiner." At least she had not squeaked his name.

His charming smile answered her less than polite greeting. "Miss Sharpe. Might I have a word with you?"

Alice looked over her shoulder to see three sets of youthful eyes upon her. Her charges wore varying expressions of curiosity. She looked back to Mr. Gardiner. "I ought to attend to my charges, sir."

His gaze was direct, a gleam in his eye, and he stood back from the door with squared shoulders. "This will only take a moment of your time, and it is regarding the duke's business."

She could hardly close the door on him if he invoked the duke. Though she hesitated another moment, Alice nodded her head in agreement. "Very well." She stepped out of the door and closed it, leaving the children to their curiosity. She folded her hands over one another and attempted to appear as confident as he did.

Mr. Gardiner tilted his head slightly to the side. "I find I must apologize to you again, Miss Sharpe. In the garden the other day, when we spoke, I did not mean to offer you any slight."

"You explained that once already, Mr. Gardiner." Alice lowered her gaze to the hall carpet, which featured vines twisting and turning upon themselves. She rather felt like her insides must look as the design on the carpet did. But why? He was only a man, a guest in the duke's house. Mr. Gardiner ought not to make her feel so...so strange.

He shifted forward and bent so he could peer up into her face, startling her. "And yet you left with such haste that I knew you were fleeing my company."

Alice's eyes narrowed as she backed up a step. "If this is why you have disturbed my time with the children—"

"It isn't. Not entirely." He offered what he likely thought a charming grin. While Alice readily admitted he was attractive, she squelched any desire to give in to him merely due to his looks.

"Well then." She lifted her chin, glaring at him through the lenses of her spectacles. "You invoked His Grace a moment ago. What might I do for the duke?"

His wide grin diminished into a bemused frown. "The project —my catalog of insects and flora in the duke's gardens—that is the business I meant."

Alice suppressed a sigh, reminding herself to be patient. This man was the duke's guest. She could not simply dismiss him for bringing up the subject. "As I said, sir, I have enough work to do for the duke and duchess through tutoring their children. I cannot spare time to assist you."

"What if the duke specifically allowed it?" Mr. Gardiner asked.

Frost formed along Alice's spine, making her stiffen with dread. "You have not spoken to him about the idea, surely."

Mr. Gardiner misinterpreted her tone as surprised rather than mortified, given the way his smile sprang back into place. "I told him what I saw in your sketchbook. You have a deft hand, and you have the talent of a professional colorist. We spoke after dinner last evening."

The man had such confidence in what he had proposed that he went to the duke! Alice clenched her hands together and tightened her jaw. From the moment the position of governess settled upon her, scant days before, Alice wanted only to keep out of sight and out of mind. The duke was powerful, and no one from her expansive family resided nearby. If he cast her off, she doubted anyone would wish to accept her back into their homes.

Alice loosened her jaw enough to speak. "You spoke to the duke. About me."

For the first time, Mr. Gardiner appeared less certain of himself. "I did. Because you have a talent, Miss Sharpe. A talent that I find useful, and that could have your name appear in a scientific publication."

She wrapped one arm around her stomach. "Mr. Gardiner, please tell me what was said by you, and by his grace. I need to understand the situation."

For the duke's attention to bear on her for something as simple as her flower drawings—it made that icy feeling in her spine leak through to her limbs.

People were dismissed from positions like hers with less reason than Mr. Gardiner had given the duke. Her whole focus ought to be the children. The list of rules given to her by the dowager duchess and the Duchess Montfort had included many things. Among them had been fraternizing with male staff members, male neighbors, and any other gentleman with more on his mind than what politeness demanded. They had made it clear her duty was to the children, not advancing her own social position. Not yet.

A governess to a duke might one day have her pick of gentlemen, when all the children grew past the age of needing her. If someone had the wrong idea about Mr. Gardiner's interest in her—

"I make a report to his grace on my progress, almost daily. Last evening, I mentioned coming upon you and Lord James in the gardens." He spoke slowly, as though she were a child incapable of understanding the situation. Horrid man. It was *he* who did not know what trouble this might cause Alice. "I told him I saw your sketches and the coloring you did of one subject. Your talent impressed me, and I mentioned that it might help my project to have someone like you to assist with the illustrations of plants. To check my work and color the designs."

A tiny ray of hope entered Alice's heart. "You did not suggest that I specifically fulfill that role?"

"I did not." He glowered down his nose at her. Before she could feel relief, before she could retreat to the safety of the schoolroom, he spoke again. "The duke, however, suggested that I ask you to perform the task if it doesn't interfere with your work as a governess."

The duke had made a suggestion. Most in the kingdom would know well enough it may as well be a command. Alice, an orphaned daughter of a gentleman, penniless and dependent on her family or her ability to find employment, could not afford to do anything that might disappoint a man of such power. While the duchess had given Alice employment, Her Grace would expect obedience to the duke.

This left Alice rather stuck.

She handled the situation with as much dignity as she could.

"Then I suppose you have your answer, Mr. Gardiner. If His Grace wishes for me to assist you, I will of course make time to lend my skill to your work."

Mr. Gardiner's dark eyebrows pulled together, a sharp V appearing above his nose. "Miss Sharpe—"

Another voice said her name at nearly the same moment. "Miss Sharpe, Mr. Gardiner, have I arrived in time for tea?"

Mr. Gardiner moved aside, already mid-bow, revealing Miss Arlen standing behind him. When she had come upon them in the corridor, Alice did not know. She had been too distressed to give heed to anything other than the presumptuous gentleman standing before her.

How had she ever considered him charming?

"A pleasure to see you this morning, Miss Arlen," Mr. Gardiner said, all politeness.

"Thank you, Mr. Gardiner." Miss Arlen's clever brown eyes darted to Alice's, then back to Mr. Gardiner. Her lips pressed together a moment, as though she was making sense of the scene she had come upon. "Are you joining us for tea?"

"No," Alice said before the gentleman could answer. "He has only come to speak to me about his insects, and now he must be on his way." Although she did not precisely mean to sound upset, she did not sound approving, either. The rudeness of sending the man on his way made her feel momentary guilt.

Miss Arlen shivered. "Ah yes, the project for the duke. I cannot say it is a topic I know much about." The well-mannered companion sounded apologetic. "But I do understand the importance of the subject."

Mr. Gardiner's smile tightened. He bowed again. "I thank you for that much, Miss Arlen. As Miss Sharpe has said, I must excuse myself. I have things to attend to before this evening."

Alice caught a puzzled frown from him the instant before he turned away to walk down the corridor to the main staircase. She watched his retreating form for several moments until Miss Arlen shifted to stand beside her.

The two of them watched him for a beat before Miss Arlen spoke. "He is a handsome gentleman, to be certain. But can you imagine being married to a man who brings boxes of insects into his rooms?" She shook her head. "I would have nightmares of them escaping."

Alice nearly snorted a laugh but kept it back. Barely.

Miss Arlen's eyes danced, and she wrinkled her pixie nose. "You do not mind insects, I take it?"

"Not overmuch." But the gentleman studying the crawling creatures had unexpectedly proven problematic. Alice gestured to the closed door behind them. "Our tea will arrive soon, and I made certain the kitchen knew to send up enough for a guest."

Miss Arlen's steps were light and buoyant as she walked into the schoolroom. She took in everything with an alertness she had not possessed the day before. "I realized yesterday," said she, "that it has been ages and ages since I spent more than a moment in this room. Lady Josephine and I had another five years left of schooling when this room was opened to us, ten years ago now."

Lady Isabelle and Lady Rosalind had apparently put away their things in preparation for tea. Lord James had left the table to set up a row of tin soldiers along one of the shelves.

"Emma," Lady Isabelle said brightly. "I am glad you're here."

"As am I," Lady Rosalind said chirpily, coming forward with arms extended for a hug. Obviously, Lady Josephine's companion was well liked and most familiar with the family. The young noblewomen immediately set up a chatter, asking questions about the guests from the dinner the night before.

"Now, you know your mother does not like gossip." Miss Arlen took a chair at the large round table. "You must put your minds at rest. The adults spoke about adult things, such as politics and matchmaking, and that is all you need know."

"Matchmaking?" Lady Rosalind asked, batting her eyelashes. "Who is matchmaking?"

"Everyone, of course. If people are not talking about politics or fashion, they are speaking of marriages, which require both." Miss Arlen's laugh dismissed the topic at once. "I am not here to rehearse the dinner conversation with you. I wish to know Miss Sharpe better."

Both girls blinked as though surprised, but their brother spoke the thought they obviously had. "But she's just the governess."

A flash of memories flooded Alice's mind and heart, memories of aunts and cousins, grandmothers and uncles, all muttering something along the lines of, *Oh, it's only Alice.*

She cleared her throat. And the sting of a hundred dismissals. It took her a moment to form words, to try and find what to say that would not sound like a weak defense of her position.

Thankfully, someone else knew precisely what to say.

Miss Arlen's previously cheerful expression had changed to one of compassion, and no little amount of understanding. "I am just your sister's companion, James. Not anyone of great importance, by many standards, and yet I have the ear of the duke's eldest daughter. Miss Sharpe, though employed by your family, has your parents' trust along with her solemn responsibility to tutor the three of you." She gestured to include the silent sisters in the conversation. "Who do you think educates the ruling class in our society? Who teaches a king his letters or a duke his first sums? Governesses and tutors. Without them, I think you should turn out rather poorly."

At that moment, Miss Arlen gained a firm friend in Alice. The elegant woman had responded better than Alice could have, and with such understanding and empathy. Her every word rang with truth and reason.

Lord James, his chin tucked against his chest, did not quite meet Alice's eye when he mumbled an apology to her. "I am sorry for my thoughtless words, Miss Sharpe."

"All is forgiven, Lord James."

Thankfully, the maid assigned to the nursery arrived at that moment with a heavily laden tea tray. Once everyone had been served, Miss Arlen proved to be the perfect guest. She was lively, polite, and seemed genuinely interested in coming to know Alice better.

Despite the concern caused by Mr. Gardiner's proposition, Alice tentatively hoped she had found a friend in Miss Arlen.

CHAPTER 8

Normally, Rupert could count on offering a smile and kind word as enough to win him favor from a lady. Not that he sought such attention often, given that his studies consumed most of his time. Most women viewed his interest in insects as a perplexing hobby at best, and a disgusting obsession at worst.

Conversely, Miss Sharpe had seemed intrigued by entomology, but rather put off by *him*.

Curious.

Rupert lay stretched across the grass, sketching a leaf and the leaf-shaped beetle sitting upon it, while he considered the problem at hand.

In his attempts to soothe her concerns, Rupert had distressed her. How had that happened? She insisted his suggestion did not offend her, yet she resisted the idea of helping him. Perhaps he had completely misread her interest.

The shield beetle steadily climbed up his leaf onto the stem of the flower. Though he admired the insect's ingenuity, he should report it to the head gardener. Agriculturally, shield bugs were pests, considering their voracious appetite for tender leaves.

He closed his sketchbook and crossed his arms upon the grass, resting his chin upon his forearm. His coat he'd cast aside somewhere behind him when he had first started hunting in the flowerbed for a different specimen to draw. It was too hot, and too impractical, to wear the coat while hunting insects.

As a man of science, he often wondered why so much of what humankind did had no practical reasoning behind it. While he bowed to convention most of the time, as one in his position must, Rupert bent the rules when they made little sense. Such as wearing stuffy, warm layers while spending time in the sun's heat.

He had sent a note to Miss Sharpe to meet him in the gardens at her earliest convenience. It was nearing three in the afternoon and she had not yet appeared. Given his previous encounters with the governess, he had thought she might seek him out earlier.

Rupert rolled onto his back and tucked his hands behind his head, closing his eyes against the sunlight. Rather like a lizard, he enjoyed the warmth for several long moments while considering where to search for a new subject to draw.

A shadow fell across his face. Then a soft voice spoke.

"Mr. Gardiner? Are you sleeping?"

He opened one eye, then squinted upward with both. Miss Sharpe had arrived at last. Today she wore a wide straw bonnet, a gown of muted rose with a plain fichu tucked and gathered to cover every inch of skin nearly up to her chin.

"Ah, Miss Sharpe. Here you are." He sat up, and she hastily stepped backward, putting an unnecessary amount of distance between them. "I had nearly given up hope of seeing you today."

He noted that she clutched the handle of a basket in one hand and a book in the other. Her jaw appeared rather taut, and there were spots of color in her cheeks. "I am afraid the children were somewhat quarrelsome today, so our studies took extra time. Then I was required to join them in their music and art lessons, as their instructors needed assistance. But here I am at last, while the children take tea with their mother and grandmother."

Quarrelsome children might explain her somewhat lackluster

disposition. "I am sorry to hear about the children. I imagine it is difficult to remain inside at lessons with so many other amusements at hand."

Her eyes narrowed. "Perhaps." Then she squared her shoulders. "Your note did not say precisely what you wished to discuss, but as we are in the garden, I assumed you wished me to begin as your colorist." She bent to put her basket down, then opened her book and took a pencil from inside it. "If you will tell me what you require, I will make note of it before we begin."

Although he normally admired individuals who came straight to the point, as he much preferred to do the same, her manner bordered on brusque. Obviously, the woman still bore contempt for either his person or the project at hand.

Her gaze darted up from the page to his arms, then up to his eyes, before she dropped them again to the book.

Had his lack of coat offended her?

Although it would be an easy matter to slip the heavy cloth on again, Rupert did not move to find it. If they were to spend time together, she would have to accustom herself to how he went about his work.

"What I require, Miss Sharpe, is a meeting of the minds." Rupert had the satisfaction of seeing her eyebrows lift, her eyes coming up to his filled with skepticism. "And while I have apologized multiple times for giving offense, it is obvious you still harbor some ill feeling toward me. If that is the case, I fail to understand why you are standing here at all."

As he spoke, her eyes narrowed to slits and her chin lifted. "I am standing here, sir, because my employer expects it. Or do you think one as insignificant as I am can ignore the preferences of a duke?" The sharpness in her tone surprised him. As did her perspective of the situation.

"You truly have no wish to be a part of a scientific study?" Rupert dropped his arms to his side. "But you seemed so interested—and you have a natural talent—"

"Thank you." She sighed and wrapped both hands around her book. "But the flattery is unnecessary. I am afraid I cannot spare more than an hour, then I must attend to the children again. Will you please tell me, sir, what it is you need me to do?"

Although uncertain as to why she was still upset, Rupert bent to retrieve his book from the ground. "As I said before, the process of preparing this catalog for the duke is more arduous and time consuming than I expected. I can render an insect in near perfect detail, and the coloration of the creatures is important to me. The flowers and plants where they make their bowers or their dinners are no less important. They need to be rendered in excellent detail."

He flipped open his sketchbook and took a loose sheet of paper out, showing it to her. "Here is the plant from the pond where we met, the same one you were drawing."

She looked from his picture up to him. "Yes. Your drawing and mine show similar skill."

"But I haven't the time to color it in while I am also working on producing the seven different insects I found living upon the loosestrife." He stared hard at her, trying to convey his need through his stare alone. "I will draw everything, Miss Sharpe, and deliver the flowers to you. If you would lend me your talent of making them look *real*, with vivid and accurate color, I will forever be in your debt. The duke intends to publish what I am compiling into a book for himself, but we will also submit it for scientific publication."

"Then what does it matter if my colors are correct?" she asked, arching her blonde eyebrows at him, one corner of her mouth pulling aside skeptically. "The publishing houses will have their own colorists—"

"And those colorists must copy from an original. Your work will be the original colors." How could he help her understand how important it was to him? "Please, Miss Sharpe. Accuracy is of great importance, to His Grace and to me."

She studied his drawing again, almost reluctantly. "What about the insects?"

Perhaps she was more bothered by multi-legged, miniscule creatures than he had thought. "I will color them in."

"Very well." She handed the drawing back to him, then scribbled in her book with her pencil. He assumed she wrote his instructions, but then she tore out the paper and handed it to him. "This is what I will need to ensure accuracy. If you will note where in the garden the flower is located, I can obtain a sample to work from. I have also written the hours I will be available to you. You may either send the drawings to me or I will collect them every day." She pointed to the times she had written on the paper. "You can see that not every day is the same. Our schoolroom schedule has many variables due to the other tutors in residence and the duchess's preferences."

"Yes, I see." He had not imagined that on some days she would not have time until after the dinner hour, at eight o'clock in the evening.

She continued on, completely matter-of-fact. "If anything changes, I will let you know at once. I understand more guests are coming next week, with children and a governess of their own. That might alter circumstances, too."

Rupert's rising disappointment almost surprised him. Miss Sharpe would not spend any more time in his company than necessary. A shame. He had found her conversation interesting, her candor refreshing, and her person as a whole rather appealing.

Another glance at the paper she had given him with her list of times and instructions made his heart sink. "Suppose you have questions during the work, Miss Sharpe?"

"I will send a note." She closed her book and bent down to pick up her basket. "I promise I will be as efficient as possible."

Efficiency hadn't been quite what he hoped for, but Rupert nodded in reluctant acceptance. "May I ask—" He cut himself off, realizing he had no way to politely inquire as to whether or not she disliked his company. Not now that he had her agreement to help him.

The governess tilted her head to the side, the brim of her bonnet shading her face. "Ask...?" She let the question hang between them, her expression curious.

He dropped his gaze to her hand. "What is in your basket?"

A ridiculous question, but the best he could come up with under the circumstances.

"Oh." She removed the cloth covering. "Frogs. I think they must be ill. I found them in Lord James's room, in a trunk. I do not think he meant them any harm but keeping them indoors has done harm. I thought to take them to the sunken pond."

Rupert's jaw had fallen slack at some point. Likely when she had first shown him at least six frogs lying still atop a folded cloth. They were all breathing but hadn't made a single sound. They were likely lethargic from lack of food and water, as she had supposed.

He looked up at her. "Why—? How did—?" Then he shook his head, completely confused. Never had he spoken to a woman on the subject of insects without finding them bored or put off. But here was a woman, born and raised as a gentlewoman, who had rescued frogs from a little boy's trunk.

"I realize it would be better for the boy to return them himself, but I found them after he went out riding with his father and I thought it prudent to act in haste. I will, of course, speak to him later about this." She covered the frogs up again, and Rupert had the wild desire to swoop down and kiss her.

Instead, he gestured to the path leading down to the sunken fountain. "May I accompany you?"

Kissing a woman over her compassionate behavior toward frogs would be illogical. Especially given her rather frosty manner of a few moments before.

ALTHOUGH STILL PUT OUT WITH THE DEMANDING gentleman, Alice nodded her consent to his escort. The sunken fountain was not far. Enduring him for a few more minutes would not over-tax her.

They walked in silence at first, he with his arms tucked behind his back, still in his shirtsleeves. She kept her basket and notebook tucked tight against her stomach.

"I think I owe you another apology, Miss Sharpe."

Alice darted a look at him from the corner of her eye, around the edge of her spectacles.

"Only one, Mr. Gardiner?" She bit her tongue the moment the words escaped her. A governess could not speak to people that way.

He cocked his head to one side, and she could have sworn he fought back a smile given the way his lips tightened, and his dark eyes danced. "Perhaps several."

Alice pulled her gaze away from his, back to the path. The willow tree that acted as entrance to the sunken fountain's garden was within sight. He could not know how much his notice had harmed her comfort. "What do you imagine yourself to be apologizing for, sir?"

"Taking up your valuable time, I think. Perhaps making you uncomfortable with my demands for your help? Or maybe inconveniencing you as a whole would be the best thing to categorize the rest of my offenses beneath." He stopped walking and turned to face her, requiring her to do the same. "I am in earnest, Miss Sharpe. I did not realize until a moment ago how much my single-focus upon my task has become selfishness."

Her mouth fell open, but she hastily snapped it shut again. She had nearly agreed with him.

"I have ambition, Miss Sharpe." He tucked one arm behind his back and gestured to the garden with his other hand. "All of this might seem like no more than pretty greenery to most. Ornamental. Unimportant. But the plants and the insects living upon them are more than that. Recording them as they are now, noting how they interact with one another, might lead to remarkable discoveries one day. In my mind, I am compelled by the dizzying greatness of the future and frustrated by my own lack of understanding in the present. I am overzealous in my pursuit of discovery."

He spoke with such an earnest expression, with a weight to his words that most men reserved for the weighty matters of war and faith. His eyes burned with purpose and a passion for all that he had said. Willing her, Alice thought, to understand him.

She considered his words and weighed them against her reluctance to help him. For all that he concerned himself with the future of the world and how his research might contribute to it, he had not comprehended *her* future. Or her present.

"You have been honest with me, sir. If you will permit me to speak freely?" She hesitated, waiting for his word.

"You do not need my permission," he said instead, his brow furrowing. "A lady ought to be permitted to speak her mind."

"But I am no longer a lady of consequence, Mr. Gardiner, and therein is the problem." Alice hugged her basket closer. "Perhaps we might walk? These miserable creatures are so near the end of their suffering."

"May I?" He gestured to the basket, and Alice handed it to him. Then they continued, stepping within the curtain of the willow tree. "Speak on, Miss Sharpe. I would have us understand one another."

No one in her memory had ever treated her with such solicitude. It made her stomach twist and for a moment she forgot why she had ever been upset with him.

"I am only a woman," she said, her voice quieter than she would have liked. "I am not an amateur botanist, or entomologist, or anything else of importance. I am without important connections. My own relatives do not want me in their homes, living upon their goodwill. The path I am on is all that is available to me —the path of work, sir. My position—even if it is in one of the finest houses for one of the finest families in England—is tenuous. With no more than a thought, they could send me packing."

He appeared as though he wished to speak, to say something, but Alice hurried on. "I know the duke and duchess are honorable, good people. I have heard as much. But I should like to stay beneath their notice, and so beneath their displeasure. Taking the time away from my duties to assist you, and receiving permission from the duke in the first place to do so, has pulled me from the corner and into the center of the room."

They came through the other side of the willow to the sunny clearing and pool of water. Lord James's cobblestone faces still decorated the path beneath their feet. Dragonflies hummed along the top of the water, and a breeze mingling with distant birdsong kept the air from growing too quiet or too still.

Mr. Gardiner lowered the basket to the ground beside the sunken fountain. "It is not that you do not wish to help, then. But that you do not want the attention it brings upon you."

Alice nodded tightly, not looking at him as she knelt beside the basket. She began removing her gloves as she spoke. "I have always tried to make myself useful. I enjoy drawing, and painting, and flowers are a fine subject. But if being useful to your work puts my place as governess in peril—"

"It will not." He came to his knees, too, and caught her hand before she could remove the cloth from the basket. She forced herself to raise her gaze to his. The earnest expression in his deep brown eyes nearly compelled her to believe him. "And if you believe the risk is too great, you have but to tell me and I will intercede on your behalf. Or—" His cheeks reddened, and he lowered his gaze to their hands. He removed his rather slowly. "Or you may withdraw your assistance now, Miss Sharpe. I will make it right with His Grace, if you wish to forget the whole of it."

She took the cloth off the top of the frogs, then stared down into it for a long moment. They were so still. Barely moving even to breathe. The poor things had been trapped too long indoors, away from their home and all that they knew. She tipped the basket slowly on its side, forcing the animals inside to move and then catch themselves upon the grass.

They started at once for the water, some faster than the others, but all perked up the moment she took the basket away. She only had to give one an extra nudge with her finger, and it surprised her by leaping farther than the rest, into the water.

Alice could not stop herself from smiling as the little creatures paddled around, then disappeared beneath the surface. They would recover, and she would teach Lord James the importance of leaving creatures in their natural homes.

"They are surprisingly delicate creatures, frogs."

Alice glanced from the corner of her eye at the gentleman beside her. "Indeed, sir."

He turned his expectant gaze back to her. "And yet, resilient enough to spend as much time underwater as a fish, for all that they lack gills and breath air."

She nearly smiled at that. "I suppose so."

He picked up the basket and stood, offering her his hand in assistance. Alice considered his bare palm a moment before placing her own inside of it, her gloves tucked into her notebook.

"You have yet to tell me if I am forgiven, Miss Sharpe." He spoke softly, his hand still holding hers. "If I must earn your good favor—"

The moment had turned too tense, too serious, for a governess and a gentleman. Alone. In a secluded garden. Mr. Gardiner possessed no little amount of charm, and he knew it. But Alice had hoped her irritation with him would make her immune to such things.

Apparently, she was as susceptible as before. Her shoulders sagged. "You are forgiven, Mr. Gardiner. You are guilty of nothing more than true dedication to your studies. How could I, a woman whose purpose is to educate others, ever disapprove?"

He brightened, his eyebrows raising and his wide smile returning. "Thank you."

"And you need not make my excuses to His Grace. I will assist in your project, as I said before." She withdrew her hand from his, folding both arms over her chest and hugging her notebook to herself. "I will do my best to help, sir."

"Only as your schedule allows." He nodded solemnly, the grin fading to something more serious. "I will not take advantage of your time unfairly. I promise."

Although Alice had a flicker of doubt over the *fairness* of the situation, she did not begrudge him the use of her time. Not really. She had read some of her cousin's scientific journals. She understood the desire to study the natural world.

As she walked back up to the castle, empty basket in hand, Alice hoped she had not agreed to more than she could reasonably manage.

CHAPTER 9

Miss Arlen arrived for tea with a new guest in tow. Alice had done no more than glimpse Lady Josephine since the night she'd had dinner with the duke's guests. When the dark-haired, graceful woman appeared in the doorway, Alice curtsied deeply.

"Lady Josephine, it is a pleasure to see you this afternoon."

The duke's eldest daughter returned the curtsy with the exceptional grace one would expect in a duke's child. "Thank you, Miss Sharpe. I do hope you will excuse my rudeness, but when Emma told me how much she enjoyed your company, I had to come and make your acquaintance."

Alice darted a glance at Miss Arlen, whose tight-lipped smile and dancing eyes suggested her amusement rather than any regret.

"That is most kind of Miss Arlen." She looked over her shoulder where the children were gathered. One side of the large schoolroom was set up rather like a parlor, to encourage the children and teach them how best to behave in such a setting. They would take their tea there.

When the children caught sight of their sister, they visibly brightened.

"Josie, you've come to take tea with us?" Lord James asked, bouncing to the edge of his chair.

"We thought you would be with Mother and Grandmama." Lady Isabelle moved to the far side of her couch and patted the seat next to her in clear invitation.

Lady Josephine came into the room and sat between Lady Isabelle and Lady Rosalind. She put one arm around each of them in a brief embrace. "I had much rather be here, especially since there are no guests to entertain at present. Next week things will be different again. But here I might nibble on cakes without Grandmama remarking on what they might do to my figure."

The girls laughed, and Lord James bounced again in his chair. "We have such good cakes, too. Miss Sharpe doesn't mind it like the *last* governess."

Despite her soldier-like stance, Alice returned his grateful grin. "I should not like to have bread and butter with my tea every day. I cannot imagine why children should have to do so." She looked to Miss Arlen, whose relaxed posture gave Alice leave to stand at her ease.

Perhaps she need not fear Lady Josephine's scrutiny as she thought she must, but wisdom dictated that she tread carefully. "Do sit, Miss Arlen. The tea will be here in a few moments, I'm certain."

"Thank you." Miss Arlen drifted to one of the remaining empty chairs. "Lady Josephine and I were discussing the deplorable lack of women our own age in the last round of guests. There were any number of matrons, and a few of their sons, but no unmarried women."

Had they come in search of more company? Alice lowered herself into her favorite chair—a battered gray seat modeled after Queen Charlotte's sitting room chairs, she had been told. It was comfortable, for all that it bore a few scuffs from its presence in the nursery.

"I am afraid I am not much better than a matron. The children will attest to that." She gestured to the girls. "I am not the least bit amusing, am I?"

The girls giggled, trading a secretive glance with one another.

"Not amusing in the least," Lady Isabelle declared with amusement.

"Absolutely the strictest of women," Lady Rosalind put in.

Lord James pushed himself back into his chair and crossed his arms, eyes sparkling with the joke. "Dull as dishwater. That's Miss Sharpe."

Lady Josephine cocked one regal eyebrow at her younger siblings. "Dear me. Not amusing, strict, and dull. It seems Miss Arlen has misled me most terribly. What have you to say for yourself, Emma?"

The companion shrugged her delicate shoulders. "I cannot account for it, my lady. It seems I was horribly mistaken. When last I was here, Miss Sharpe made the opposite impression."

Alice clapped her hands at the performance, fighting back her own laughter. "Wonderful, children. That is precisely what you must say should anyone ask if your governess is strict enough." She cast Lady Josephine an apologetic nod. "I have told them if people think I am too wonderful, they might not believe I am doing my job properly. But we do attempt to find amusement in our studies."

"We built a pyramid out of clay yesterday," Lord James said excitedly. He jumped up from his chair and went to the cupboards lining one wall. Most were full of things for lessons, but he pulled out a baking tray with the miniature pyramid. "When it's all dry, we're to paint hieroglyphs all over it."

"We have also been reading about the deities of Egypt." Lady Isabelle said happily. "Did you know that the Greeks and Egyptians had many similar gods?"

"You sound precisely like a little heathen," Lady Josephine said, rocking back in her seat with wide eyes. "You mustn't tell Grandmama such things but *do* tell me all about it."

By the time tea arrived, the whole group discussed life upon the Nile River with as much interest as others discussed society's latest gossip. Alice poured out amid a conversation on whether Egyptian cotton was superior to the cotton grown elsewhere in the world. The topic thrilled her, reaffirming she had done something right in their studies. If the children could discuss Egypt with ease and interest, that meant they had enjoyed learning.

"Next week, our studies turn to the Romans. We will study the history, mythology, and art."

"Then I must come to tea again next week." Lady Josephine took a little cake in one hand, holding her teacup in the other. "Truly, Miss Sharpe, I wish my governess had inspired me as you have inspired these horrid little beasts."

Given the grins and giggles, the three youngest members of the duke's family enjoyed being labeled beasts by their sister. There was obvious affection among the siblings, and adoration from Alice's charges meant for their sister alone.

"They are apt pupils, my lady. We also make an effort to concentrate on the more interesting bits of history." She hid her smile behind the rim of her cup. "Other subjects are proving to be more difficult, at times. We are struggling with botany."

"Oh?" Lady Josephine exchanged a surprised look with Miss Arlen. "I thought you were acquainted with our guest, Mr. Gardiner? I had heard the two of you are working together on Papa's catalog."

Alice's cheeks warmed. She had not seen Mr. Gardiner since they spoke that afternoon two days previous. Perhaps he had thought better of asking for her assistance. "We have met, and I agreed to help him when my duties allow. I cannot think of disturbing him with the children's lessons."

Miss Arlen's teacup rattled against her saucer. "Why ever not? If you are to help him, he ought not mind helping you."

Lady Josephine gave a succinct nod. "I quite agree. It would be ungentlemanly of him to refuse."

Lord James had wandered away to a row of soldiers upon the table, and Lady Rosalind had taken up a book to read while she nibbled on a molasses biscuit. That left Lady Isabelle as part of their conversation, sitting precisely the way her elder sister sat.

"I do not think he would refuse, should I ask him. But I have no wish to put anyone out on my account." Alice shifted in her chair, lowering her eyes to the carpet. "Mr. Gardiner's work for His Grace is of great importance. Taking time away from that work for the children to learn more about flowers seems frivolous."

Lady Josephine persisted, leaning forward almost eagerly. "Given that botany is such an important subject to Papa, and that Mr. Gardiner is something of an expert, I doubt it would be seen that way."

Why the duke's eldest daughter felt so strongly on the matter, Alice could not guess. But Miss Arlen nodded along sagely with every word. Perhaps the entire household shared the duke's obsession with plants.

A knock on the door prohibited Alice from making her answer. She rose from where she sat and went to the door, puzzled. Had the schoolroom become the center of household socializing?

Alice opened the door to reveal three maids, two bearing large, ornate pots full of flowers. The flowers were in every color imaginable, with two of each type of blossom, appearing rather like colorful explosions in the arms of the servants.

"What is all this?" Alice asked. The strong fragrance of several types of flowers wafted through the hall and into the schoolroom.

The maid without flowers handed Alice a folded sheet of paper, torn along the edge as though it had come out of a book. She held in her other arm a sheaf of paper tucked against her chest. Alice unfolded the note and read it, and with each word her heart beat faster.

Miss Sharpe,

Here are the first blossoms. I've made note of their names and where they were found in the gardens on this paper. If you feel any of my sketches need correction, know that I trust your judgement on the matter and do not hesitate to mend my mistakes.

Please have the sketches returned to me when you are finished with them.

Thank you for your efforts.

Most Sincerely,

R.G.

She stepped out of the doorway and gestured for the maids to enter. "Do put those on the table. Thank you for bringing them all the way upstairs." The maid with the papers held them out, and Alice took them. She leafed through each sheet, noting the charcoal and pencil sketches of several flowers, all without color.

There were perhaps two dozen sheets.

"Have you an admirer, Miss Sharpe?" Lady Josephine had risen to examine the flowers. The maids curtsied and filed out the door, closing it behind them. "If so, he ought to be informed that mixing this many blooms is more likely to cause a headache than tenderness of feeling."

"The orchids are rather strong," Miss Arlen agreed. "But very pretty."

Alice came to the table and put the stack of paper upon its surface, then handed Lady Josephine the note. "Not an admirer, my lady. Mr. Gardiner."

What did the *R* stand for?

"Oh, this is part of the catalog project." Lady Isabelle had flounced her way over to the table, too. "You have to paint all of these?" Her eyes widened at the task.

Alice looked again at the drawing on the top of the stack. "I am expected to do my best, yes." She lifted it to inspect the next one.

"You see, the gentleman owes you a favor." Lady Josephine sounded rather triumphant as she handed the note back to Alice. "You will make your best effort on his behalf, so he will do the same for you."

As though used to echoing her lady, Miss Arlen immediately agreed. "You can at least ask him, Miss Sharpe."

Alice shook her head, reading his note once more, her eyes tracing the curls of his handwriting as well as its sharp points. The R continued to intrigue her.

"Perhaps you are right. If an opportunity presents itself, I will speak to him."

From the corner of her eye, she thought she detected Lady Josephine and Miss Arlen sharing suspiciously pleased grins. But she had to have imagined it. What did they truly care if she spoke to Mr. Gardiner or not?

Alice had more pressing issues. She had two dozen types of flowers to paint.

CHAPTER 10

R upert dug about in his largest trunk, hunting for a book on the subject of bees. He had found a large swarm in the lower gardens and meant to discover exactly where they had come from and where they might go next. The beekeeper on the estate knew nothing of the swarm and swore not a single one of his hives had abandoned their posts. He seemed keen to add new bees to his colonies, however.

"I am uncertain we brought your book on beekeeping, sir." Billings stood by, stoic as ever, with several starched cravats in hand. "But since you are here, perhaps you would choose your jacket for dinner this evening?"

"My choice of clothing is not nearly as important as those bees." Rupert came out of the trunk and fussed with his hair, trying to get it out of his face. "They do not look at all like the bees kept on the castle grounds. I think they are a different breed entirely. I have asked the beekeeper about catching them."

Billings simply stared at him, cravats still in hand.

The valet assisted Rupert with insects when required but had no interest in them on his own. With a sigh, Rupert gestured to the closet. "The blue jacket, then."

"Very good, sir." The valet turned with his cravats, apparently intending to stow them away, when he paused. "I nearly forgot to tell you, sir, but Miss Sharpe sent back your drawings. They are upon your desk."

"She did?" Rupert brightened at once and rushed to the desk. A stack of papers waited for him, with a half sheet on top of the whole. He held it at an angle to read with the low evening light.

Mr. Gardiner,

I have given your sketches color, to the best of my ability. I apologize for the time I took to complete the task, but with the arrival of the new guests, my time has been limited. I hope you find my work satisfactory.

Miss A. Sharpe

A numbered list below her note labeled the flowers.

The sketches had gone to her four days previous. *Four days.* She had worked with more speed than he had thought possible. How had she done it so swiftly?

He took up two of the papers and held them to the light, studying the colors carefully. Each drawing had a small number in one corner, corresponding to the name of the flower on the list Miss Sharpe had sent.

"Beautiful," he murmured, noting the unique orange of the Welsh poppy, the delicate shading of white Ground-elder. Wildflowers and those planted and cultivated by the groundskeeping staff were each given the same amount of care.

"I take it you are pleased with her work, sir?" Billings sounded disinterested, but when Rupert glanced up, he saw his valet's eyes had narrowed.

"Very pleased. She has a perfect eye for color and an artist's hand. Look at these."

Billings came closer and accepted one of the papers. He hummed with feigned interest. "It is lucky you found out about her talent."

"Indeed." Rupert took up several more sheets, sifting through them. "Her work is stunning."

"You ought to tell her that, sir." Billings put his paper back in the pile. "It does a soul good to know when their work is appreciated."

"You are right, of course." Rupert put the papers down and clapped his valet on the shoulder. "As you well know. Thank you, Billings. I will find her and give Miss Sharpe her due." He glanced out the window. "After my work is done today."

Rupert had left most of his things outside, near the edge of the forest where he had caught sight of the bees.

He really needed better organization. And to send to his home, sixteen miles away, for his beekeeping book.

Striking out for the gardens with a wide-brimmed straw hat upon his head, Rupert walked with purpose. He knew his way around well enough, and cut through hedges and around a folly, thinking only of his various tools, nets, and sketchbook waiting for him.

Or trying to think only on those things.

Keeping his mind busy upon his task kept it away from his curiosity about Miss Sharpe. He hadn't seen her in nearly a week and truly began to despair of ever seeing her again.

The number of guests in the house had tripled the amount of people at dinner. And the table was, unfortunately, too well balanced for anyone to think of sending for the governess.

Thankfully, since the duke made it clear that Rupert had much to occupy his time, no one expected him to be about to entertain anyone. Though there were two young women at dinner the evening before who had shown more than a passing interest in coming to know him. *That* would likely change the moment the duke's eldest child, his son and heir, arrived for the house party.

Truthfully, it was the presence of the unattached ladies that had sent him to the far reaches of the castle gardens. He had no wish for husband-hunting females to come in search of him.

A scream of laughter caused Rupert to falter in his step. A shout of dismay followed the laughter, and then sounds of distress from several voices assaulted him.

What sort of gentleman would he be to keep walking? It sounded as though something dreadful had happened on the other side of an ivy-covered wall. Rupert sighed, tugged the brim of his hat lower, and went directly for the wall. He put his hands atop it, then heaved himself up.

Sitting on the wall, a leg over each side, Rupert looked down into the garden. The plants and flowers cultivated in that area were all imports from the Far East. The head gardener had put them into a walled garden to avoid creating hybrids with English flowering plants.

Several children of various ages were standing in a circle beneath a tree, all looking down. Two women, dressed in severely dark gowns and wearing sour expressions upon pale faces, stood on the edges of the circle.

And in the circle itself, which Rupert could barely make out even from his higher position, Miss Sharpe knelt on the ground with a child half in her arms.

Rupert dropped down into the garden and hastened to her side. "Excuse me, children. Please, stand back. Give the little one some room." He spoke firmly, and found the children hastening to obey. The sour-faced women relaxed their glares and one of them directed the children to the other side of the garden.

Miss Sharpe looked up at him, her face pale and eyes burning with what he assumed to be anger—but where was that anger directed?

"Mr. Gardiner, thank goodness you are here. Geoffrey fell out of the tree, and I cannot move him on my own. I think we must send for a doctor."

The one remaining sour woman huffed. "I am certain the lad is fine. He is forever getting into scrapes. He will rouse and be well."

Given the way Miss Sharpe's eyes narrowed at that declaration, Rupert knew he had found the source of her anger. He addressed himself to that woman. "Thank you for your opinion, Miss...?"

The matronly woman drew herself up. "Miss Felton. I am the governess for Baron Addington's children." She added, almost as an afterthought, "And Geoffrey."

Ah, one of the guests had brought a governess along with his brood. Rupert nodded to her. "Thank you, Miss Felton. I know the duke has a fondness for children, and his honor will demand nothing less than a full examination of the child to ensure his good health. If you will excuse Miss Sharpe and I, we will take him up to the house and see to his needs, as His Grace would wish."

The woman puffed up like a hen, but she made no protests. "Very well. I will see to His Grace's children."

Miss Sharpe lowered her voice and spoke quietly to the child, whose eyes were barely open in a wince. "Geoffrey, Mr. Gardiner is going to help me get you to the house. You must try very hard to remain still while he carries you."

"Yes, Miss Sharpe." The boy's eyes closed. He was so young. He could be only five or six years old.

Rupert put one arm beneath the boy's knees and the other around his shoulders, necessitating he brush Miss Sharpe's arm as he did so. She kept her support there until he stood, making the movement easier to accomplish. The little boy groaned, turned paler still, and tucked his face against Rupert's shoulder.

Poor fellow.

Nodding to the archway on the other side of the garden, Rupert spoke quietly for the sake of the lad. "Lead the way, Miss Sharpe."

"Thank you, Mr. Gardiner." She offered him the barest of smiles before marching out of the garden at a quick pace—one that Rupert found hard to match. Before he could beg her to slow her steps, the moment they were out of the garden she waited for him and then walked alongside him.

"The poor boy knocked his head against a branch on the way down. I was watching him, though no one else noticed until he fell. His bottom came in contact with the ground first—I imagine he will be rather bruised. But he did not jump up, or even try to rouse himself, as most children do after a fall."

"A sure sign of trouble," Rupert agreed easily. "I had my own share of tumbles as a child, including one similar to this. I think it best we send for a doctor, as you suggested."

Miss Sharpe released a huff of breath. "That horrid Miss Felton said to leave him or make him stand. She said he was *pretending* the injury for attention."

Rupert grunted as he went up a wide set of steps to the next tier of gardens. "I cannot imagine the baron would like to hear his governess overlooking such a thing as a tumble out of a tree."

With lowered voice, Miss Sharpe corrected his assumption. "Geoffrey is not the baron's son. He is the son of a distant cousin. The baron is a temporary guardian."

"Still." Rupert did not understand the distinction. "The child is in his care."

"I am afraid being in someone's care is not the same as being *cared for*, Mr. Gardiner." The grim set to her jaw as she spoke those words, coupled with the sudden darkening of her eyes, made him wonder.

It put him in mind of their last conversation, when she had given him too much information, too quickly for him to respond. *My own relatives do not want me in their homes,* she had said.

"I will make certain Geoffrey is properly attended to, Miss Sharpe. I promise."

Her head turned in his direction, giving him a clear view of her lovely face and the way her lips parted, her eyes wide behind her spectacles.

Surely, his promise was not all that surprising.

But then, for a woman who openly noted the lack of care her own kin had for her, perhaps it was.

A FOOTMAN OFFERED TO RELIEVE MR. GARDINER OF Geoffrey, the boy still distressingly listless, as soon as they entered the castle. Much to her surprise, Mr. Gardiner immediately turned down that offer. Even the child's light weight would have grown burdensome by that point.

Instead, Mr. Gardiner started giving orders to the footman, and another who had appeared from the other end of the corridor.

"I will take the boy to the nursery. One of you send for the doctor, and the other must alert Lord Addington to the fellow's misadventure. Miss Sharpe, you ought to stay on hand until the doctor arrives, to answer any questions he has about the injury." He carefully adjusted his hold on the child, moving the boy higher upon his shoulder.

Geoffrey finally made a noise, the barest whimper.

The servants bowed and hastened away.

"Thank you, Mr. Gardiner," Alice whispered. "Follow me. The servants' stair will be quicker than taking the main staircase."

He fell into step behind her as she sprung open one of the hidden doors that made it possible for the servants to come and go, unseen by the duke's guests. The staircase was wide enough for two servants to pass while burdened with trays or laundry, and the steps themselves were deep enough to ensure good footing.

Not like the staircases in London that servants used. One of her uncles had a townhouse with stairs that were practically walls with shallow grooves for climbing upward. Horribly dangerous to the staff.

Alice tucked aside the nervous thought, focusing instead on her gratitude for a safe way to take the little boy to his bed.

The nursery and schoolroom were along the same corridor. By

the time they arrived there, Alice pushing open another well-concealed door, Mr. Gardiner was breathing heavily. To carry a boy, even a small one, as far as he had, and climb steps while burdened, would challenge anyone's stamina.

"We are nearly there, sir."

He did not waste breath to respond, instead he nodded tightly.

When she opened the door to the room where the little boy had a cot made up, and Mr. Gardiner brushed by her, he said not a word of complaint. He took the little fellow to the temporary bed and laid him down.

"Here we are, Master Geoffrey." The gentleman backed away at last and sat in a narrow wooden chair against the wall.

Alice hurried to remove the boy's shoes to make him more comfortable, then tucked an extra pillow beneath his head. "Are you well, Geoffrey?"

He nodded, wincing, then turned to face the wall and curled up tightly. Alice's heart ached for him. At his age, she had already learned to rarely be seen and never heard. She had already learned to keep her tears to herself, lest she upset people around her. Perhaps all orphans had to learn those lessons.

She smoothed away his curls from his forehead, as gentle as she could.

Alice went to the washstand and used the pitcher and bowl to dampen her own handkerchief. She folded it into a long rectangle, then took it to lay across the boy's forehead. Until the doctor arrived, there was nothing else to be done.

"Geoffrey, you have been very brave," Mr. Gardiner said from his place against the wall, his head tilted back, and eyes closed as he spoke. "I would have howled like a wounded pup when I was your age, lad."

That was a positive way to look at it, Alice supposed. She took up another of the chairs, a match for Mr. Gardiner's, and placed it by the boy's side. "You appear rather done in yourself, Mr.

Gardiner. If you wish to leave, I will not hold it against you. You have already done a great service."

He cracked open one eye to look at her. "I am not about to leave until I am certain our patient has been seen. To be honest, I am rather surprised the baroness hasn't appeared yet."

The little boy shifted, curling further in on himself. "They won't come."

The three whispered words bruised Alice's tender heart. She knew the truth as well as he did. "A servant will be sent to carry back news. The baroness is busy, perhaps. This is an important visit for the baron's family. A chance to strengthen their political alliances with His Grace."

Both of Mr. Gardiner's eyes opened, his expression incredulous. "Surely not—"

A knock on the doorframe interrupted his denial, and Alice turned at the same moment as he to see an older woman in the modest clothing befitting an upper servant. The baroness's maid.

"My lady sends me to look in on Master Geoffrey." She curtsied to Mr. Gardiner, then came to stand by Alice. "His Grace sent for a doctor, I am told. There is one staying nearby."

Swallowing her disappointment, Alice nodded her understanding. "You may tell Lady Addington that he is well enough for now. He has an aching head and is in poor spirits, but I am certain it will pass."

"I will inform her, of course." The maid, whose name escaped Alice in the moment, peered down at the boy and a softness stole over her features. "I will send up tea for you both and ask the cook if she might have a remedy for the boy's aching head." After another abbreviated curtsy, she left.

Mr. Gardiner's deep frown further testified that he had grown up in a better way than she. His childhood injuries and wrongs had likely been addressed with love and affection. Perhaps his mother had joined a sweet-tempered nursery maid by his bed to see to his hurts and cheer him.

He had been fortunate.

Alice brushed aside her envy. She knew well enough that the emotion served no purpose except to make her unhappy.

It is better to choose happiness over misery. She had decided upon that course long ago.

"Miss Sharpe?"

Alice turned her attention to Mr. Gardiner, adjusting her spectacles upon the bridge of her nose. "Yes?"

With a weary, crooked smile that made her heart thump a mite harder, he tipped his head to her. "Your work on the flower sketches—you are quite talented. They're remarkable likenesses. I did not expect so many in such a short time."

She tucked away a loose strand of her ash-blonde hair, averting her gaze from his. "I am glad you approve of my efforts."

"I sincerely appreciate them, as a matter of fact." He moved his chair a little closer. "Might I send you more sketches?"

Alice's heart dropped, and cold crept into her stomach. "Of course, sir." Kind as his words were, she was only a means to an end for him. As she was to everyone else.

Choose happiness.

"The flowers are all so beautiful, and I do love painting." She had enjoyed the diversion, as it had filled her evening hours after she took an early dinner with the children. As a governess, unwelcome belowstairs and in the dining room, her hours after the children went to bed were rather quiet.

Alice put her hand to Geoffrey's cheek. The little boy opened his eyes and looked up at her. "When will the doctor come, Miss Sharpe?"

The boy's voice quivered; his eyes were wide and anxious.

"I imagine in another quarter hour, if he is not very busy." She took away the cool cloth. "But you will have something to drink soon. How is your stomach? Is it upset at all?" She had seen several of her male cousins take tumbles over the years—out of trees, off horses, over furniture.

"No, miss." He shook his head a little and winced. "My head hurts a little is all."

To the best of her recollection, the injuries were never serious unless they included stomach aches and dizziness.

"I imagine it is not enjoyable to lie in bed while we two grownups talk of boring things." Mr. Gardiner chuckled and looked to Alice, a smirk upon his handsome face. He rose from his seat and crossed through the doorway to the principal part of the nursery, where the children's toys and room for them to amuse themselves lay.

Alice exchanged a bemused glance with the little boy. "Should you like to sit up a little?"

Geoffrey nodded and she helped prop up his head and neck with his small pillow.

Mr. Gardiner returned a moment later, a basket in hand. "Geoffrey, look what I've found." He knelt beside the bed and overturned the basket next to Geoffrey. "Soldiers and horses. Do you like to play soldiers?"

The boy gave the barest of nods.

"Most excellent. I always thought it rather fun to set them up in rows and columns. Plan a charge or two." He began to do that very thing, where Geoffrey could see, and handed the boy a mounted soldier. "Here is the general. He must command the troops."

With some relief, and more than a little surprise, Alice sat back in her chair and watched as Mr. Gardiner engaged the injured child in quiet play. He moved the soldiers wherever Geoffrey directed, and then began an entertaining dialogue between two of the foot soldiers.

"Did the general say to go left or right?" said one soldier, in a high voice that made Geoffrey giggle.

Mr. Gardiner gifted the other soldier with a comically deep voice. "What? But he's facing us. If he said left, was it his left or ours?"

A maid arrived with a tea tray, and instructions to give a small cup with willow bark tea and ginger to the boy, with cook's assurances it would ease his headache.

Until the doctor came, Mr. Gardiner remained, putting on quite the show with the little tin soldiers falling all over themselves to carry out their general's orders. Only when the doctor had made his examination, and pronounced that Geoffrey needed only to rest for his recovery, did Mr. Gardiner take his leave.

Alice wasn't certain who was sorrier to see him go—Geoffrey, or her.

CHAPTER 11

The next day of the house party, the children and female guests were all gathered out in a patch of garden Her Grace called "the meadow." Having seen many meadows in her life, Alice found the name more charming than accurate. Servants had perfectly mowed the grass here, and wildflowers grew in careful bunches at regular intervals along the outside of the green field. Benches strewn about a path provided comfortable seating, and the servants had brought out tables of refreshments for all to enjoy.

Alice sat beneath one of the smaller trees, upon the ground rather than a cushion, keeping a weather eye on her charges. Lady Isabelle and Lady Rosalind sat in the shade of an old oak tree, surrounded by girls near their own ages, tittering and gossiping in the way of young girls pretending to be sophisticated.

Lord James played cricket with other boys on the far side of the meadow, making up for his youth with his energy.

And closer to where the groundskeeper had directed a small stream through one end of the meadow, little Geoffrey played with the youngest children under the watchful eye of nurses and governesses alike. Truly, the servants and governesses were only present in case some calamity befell a child that their mothers did not wish to worry over.

Alice enjoyed the fresh air of the outdoors, and watching the children scamper about with their friends gave her joy as well. On beautiful afternoons such as this one, all seemed right with the world.

A voice from behind Alice startled her.

"Might we join you, Miss Sharpe?"

It was Lady Josephine and her companion, Miss Arlen.

Given that there were three other young ladies trailing behind the duke's daughter, Alice had to quell her surprise at once. Instead, she gestured to the ground near her. "You are most welcome, my lady, if you do not mind making the earth your chair."

Lady Josephine sat at once, with hardly more than a single flounce to adjust her gown's skirt, she was quite at home sitting upon the grass. The other ladies fretted a little more and appeared as bewildered as Alice was that the governess had been sought out.

"I have wanted to speak to you more about my father's project. Those flowers were beautiful, and last night at dinner, Mr. Gardiner told me how impressed he was with your skill."

One of the other women, eldest daughter to the baron, if Alice remembered correctly, gasped rather loudly. "Never say Mr. Gardiner meant *the governess* assisted him? I thought he meant some other lady of the neighborhood."

Given that "the governess" sat not five feet away, Alice wondered if the girl had ever been taught manners.

"I am afraid he meant me." Alice checked the ribbon of her straw sun bonnet, then leaned back a little more against the tree. "I am glad he found reason to be pleased with my work. I must admit, I have enjoyed the undertaking more than I thought I would."

Lady Josephine opened her mouth to speak, her eyes bright

with questions, when another of the other women released a dramatic sigh.

"Mr. Gardiner is ever so handsome. Do you get to spend much time with him?" Given the young lady's rosy cheeks, and the way her two friends started giggling, Mr. Gardiner had to be a topic of interest to them.

"Not very much at all. He sends me the sketches, and I paint in the color." Alice glanced toward Miss Arlen who appeared rather amused. "He is rather busy, I think, with collecting his own subjects to study."

"Oh, yes. The insects," the third young lady said, shuddering.

"Do forgive me." Lady Josephine snapped open her fan and gestured with her free hand to the three women who had followed her about the meadow. "I do not believe you have been properly introduced to my guests. This is Miss Finchley, Lord Addington's daughter." The baron's daughter, all prim and rosy beneath her bonnet, nodded tightly. "Miss Maria Hepsworth and Miss Hannah Hepsworth. Their father is a part of my father's political party, in the House of Commons."

The two Hepsworth sisters nodded rather proudly.

"My friends, Miss Sharpe *is* the governess for my younger sisters and brother, but I am quite comfortable saying she is a lady whose acquaintance I enjoy." Such a statement, from a duke's daughter at that, was an unqualified recommendation. And, perhaps, a warning for the others to mind their manners.

Alice did not hold back a smile of gratitude as she spoke. "You are most gracious, Lady Josephine."

Miss Arlen spoke before the ensuing silence, with the three guests appearing rather stunned, could grow awkward. "Your bonnet is most becoming, Miss Sharpe, and much more practical for the sun than my silly covering." She touched the insubstantial brim of her hat. "I do keep meaning to re-trim it. Perhaps that is something we ought to do tomorrow, my lady."

"We are looking for more amusements for ourselves," Lady

Josephine said to Alice, shrugging one shoulder. "But I do enjoy redressing bonnets. We have any number of supplies for it, too. Ribbons and silk flowers aplenty."

The conversation ebbed and flowed around Alice, with her contributing rarely. Perhaps Lady Josephine had meant it as a kindness to seek Alice out, but the Misses Hepsworths and Miss Finchley suffered no qualms in leaving Alice out of the conversation entirely.

After a time, Miss Arlen spoke directly to Alice, her tone low to avoid notice. "I do apologize, Miss Sharpe. My lady truly wished to speak to you about your work. She is a fine artist, and I think she truly admires such skills in others."

"It is no matter," Alice said softly. "If she wishes, Lady Josephine can visit me in the schoolroom. I am certain I will have more flowers and paintings very soon."

"Mr. Gardiner said many complimentary things about you," Miss Arlen added. "After dinner, in the drawing room. He is most impressed with you."

Alice's cheeks warmed. "With my painting, you mean."

Miss Arlen's eyes flashed as she tilted her head to one side. "When he spoke of the little boy you rescued—"

"Rescued?" Alice shook her head, denying the term. "Mr. Gardiner rescued him, if anyone did."

Lady Josephine had overheard their conversation and leaned in closer, leaving her friends to continue their argument over the best musician among them. "He made it sound as though you were rather essential to the child getting the care he needed."

Alice's lips parted, another protest on her tongue—

"Mr. Gardiner! Oh, do come join us." Miss Finchley trilled her welcome across the meadow.

Alice turned her gaze in that direction and saw him, tall and dark haired, wearing a brown coat and long trousers tucked into dark boots. His arms were full of a large basket, several long nets, and the hat that had apparently fallen off his head. He hesitated where he stood, staring at their gathering beneath the tree.

Lowering her head, Alice hid beneath the brim of her bonnet, silently wishing he would walk on. Yet something in her chest fluttered rather like that green and white butterfly she had caught during their first meeting when she heard Miss Hepsworth hiss, "He is coming."

WHILE RUPERT MUCH PREFERRED TO ACT AS THOUGH HE HAD not heard the summons of Miss Finchley, his glimpse of *another* person sitting beneath the tree gave him pause. Though she lowered her head at once, Rupert knew well the shape of her shoulders and the way she turned her head.

Miss Sharpe.

For her, he would cross the meadow.

Curious. Until that moment, Rupert had not realized he knew her mannerisms well enough to identify her from afar, as easily as he might identify a honeybee among wasps in the heather. Perhaps his time spent with her in the nursery the day before had influenced that knowledge.

His eyes sought the children down by the stream, and it took him a moment to identify the curly head of their former patient. But how did Miss Sharpe fare, now that the little boy jumped about happily with his fellows?

Arms still laden with his supplies, and a basket for the gathering of more flowers for Miss Sharpe, Rupert barely avoided a stray cricket ball hurtling through the grass, then twisted about when several boys slightly taller than his elbow whisked by him with cricket bats. Apparently, there was a question as to whether it had gone out of bounds.

"Ladies." He greeted them with a bow before depositing his things upon the ground. "Might I join you a moment?"

"Only a moment, Mr. Gardiner?" Miss Finchley asked, eyelashes fluttering more rapidly than a butterfly on the wing.

Perhaps this hadn't been a good idea.

Lady Josephine spoke before he could retract the request. "Of course, sir. I am certain you welcome a moment's respite from the task my father has set you." She shared with him a familiar smile—the one she had used since girlhood to set others at ease. Though he was several years her senior, Rupert appreciated her efforts.

All but one lady looked upon him with expressions varying from curious to openly flirtatious.

Miss Sharpe kept her gaze down, ostensibly adjusting her gloves and the sketchbook in her lap.

Had she grown shy? But why?

Rupert tried a casual beginning to their conversation. "How is our patient today, Miss Sharpe? He appears quite merry by the stream."

Her chin barely lifted, just enough for her gaze to meet his before she glanced over to the stream where nurses watched the younger children play. "I do not think he even remembers the hurt, given how happily he is splashing the others around him."

"Children are resilient little beasts." Rupert tilted his head to one side, studying her profile. She had delicate features he could not help but admire, and the frames of her spectacles highlighted the bright blue of her eyes rather nicely.

"Mr. Gardiner," Miss Hannah said, voice louder than strictly necessary given their proximity. "How much longer do you think your work will take? Will you still be here during the duchess's summer ball in a week?"

The accursed ball. He had nearly forgotten about that. Forcing a lightness to his tone, Rupert answered with a nod. "I believe I will be here long after the rest of you have left for home. I have cataloged approximately one-third of the area His Grace was most interested in. Of course, things should go somewhat faster now that I have Miss Sharpe's talent added to my own efforts."

Miss Hepsworth spoke quickly, almost as though she wished to cover his words with her own. "Thank goodness you will be here, Mr. Gardiner. My sister and I were discussing how few people we know in this part of the country. I can scarcely believe there are enough people of good breeding to fill the ballroom."

Rupert caught the way Miss Sharpe lowered her head at this, and he sensed her quiet withdrawal from the conversation. As governess, she likely believed herself unable to contribute to the topic of balls.

Lady Josephine's light laugh dismissed whatever slight Miss Hepsworth may have meant. "I assure you, there are many gentlemen and ladies in our county who see my mother's ball as the very height of summer festivities. People travel some hours to come and dance the evening away. Then they ride off in the morning, half-sleeping, to their homes." She turned to Rupert, her dark eyes bright with something other than good humor. "Is it not so, Mr. Gardiner? You have attended several such balls in the past."

"The ball is always a grand occasion," he admitted, still watching Miss Sharpe from the corner of his eye. "All the doors and windows are thrown open, the gardens are filled with lanterns and torchlight, and there is not room enough for every couple to dance every set. The midnight supper is a feast, and everyone stays until the sun creeps up over the horizon."

Still, Miss Sharpe did not look his way.

"I am delighted we are guests in the castle this year," Miss Finchley said, genuine excitement upon her face.

Every year during the summer months, the duke and duchess hosted several house parties. Their guests varied from year to year, so it was no wonder the baron and Mr. Hepsworth's families had never attended before. Their country seats were in different counties.

"Will you tell us more about the flowers you are studying, Mr. Gardiner?" Miss Arlen, the companion to the duke's daughter, shifted somewhat closer to the quiet governess as she spoke. "Miss

Sharpe has not shared much detail with us yet, though I am fascinated by her part in your work."

Lady Josephine swiftly seconded her companion's choice of topic. "Oh, yes. I have so many questions. Do you intend to give color to all the flowers you find? And illustrate them all?"

Once more, Rupert looked away from studying the far-too-quiet governess. "For His Grace's personal catalog, yes." He gestured to Miss Sharpe. "For the publication I will submit to the Royal Society, Miss Sharpe will have to help me pick the illustrations of the most interest."

Her gaze came up at that, and her eyebrows lifted above the rims of her spectacles. "I am certain you do not need my help for that, sir."

"You must have some say in it, given that your name will appear upon the publication, credited as the colorist."

Her cheeks pinked rather prettily. "But I hardly know what others in your field of study will find most interesting."

Rupert leaned slightly toward her, despite the five-foot gap between where they sat. "You have seen the sorts of flowers that are in scientific journals and pamphlets. You also know what level of skill is necessary to render certain plants perfectly. I will depend upon your eye and talent, Miss Sharpe."

One corner of her lips turned upward, but before a full smile appeared, Miss Finchley started chirping with all the tenacity of one of his father's beloved parrots.

"Mr. Gardiner, how wonderful that you will be published by the Royal Society. My father is a great admirer of their work, and indeed has considered becoming a patron, but then the Regent himself patronizes the Royal Society, does he not?" She spoke with a rapidity that allowed no one else to comment for several moments, going on at length about the sciences. Most of what she said was nonsense. But she finished with her eyelashes batting at him again. "I do so admire a man of intelligence, Mr. Gardiner. What first interested you in the sciences?"

"My father is an ornithologist," he said, mentally trying to find a way to extract himself from the conversation. "I grew up surrounded by his studies, and so began my own."

"Ornithology?" Miss Hepsworth exchanged a glance with her sister, then Miss Finchley. "What branch of study is that?"

"The science of birds," Miss Sharpe said. Nearly at the same moment Rupert gave that exact answer.

She met his surprised gaze with her own, the barest smile touching her lips again.

Miss Hepsworth looked from Rupert to Miss Sharpe, her nose wrinkling. "How fascinating."

"I cannot say I ever had a governess clever enough to know such things," Miss Finchley said with a sniff. She cut a cold glance toward Miss Sharpe, an obvious attempt to put the governess in her place.

Rupert resisted the desire to run. He had seen enough women begin verbal attacks to sense one coming. He could not come to her defense without making the moment more awkward, having already praised her.

Miss Sharpe blushed and dropped her gaze to her lap again.

Rupert rather wished to throttle Miss Finchley.

Lady Josephine snapped her fan open with the same air with which a man might draw his sword. "We are most fortunate that Mother and Grandmama discovered Miss Sharpe. Every time I visit the nursery, I am delighted by what I learn in my conversations with her."

The duke's daughter had drawn a line in the sand with those words. Marking Miss Sharpe as an above-average person in both her career and the lady's esteem.

"I quite agree," Rupert said firmly. He stood. "But if you do not mind, Lady Josephine, I should like to steal Miss Sharpe away for a moment. I must show her some variation in one of the flowers I am studying to get her opinion for the catalog. Excuse us, ladies."

He bowed, at the same moment holding his hand out to Miss Sharpe. There was no room for argument, and if they moved swiftly enough, no one else might invite themselves along.

"Of course, Mr. Gardiner." Miss Sharpe put her gloved hand in his, and with a quick tug he helped her up to her feet. "Good day, Lady Josephine. Ladies."

Miss Sharpe curtsied, then beat him to scooping up his butterfly nets.

Rupert recovered the rest of his equipment, then gestured with a tip of his head across the meadow. "That way, Miss Sharpe. Toward the forest, if you will."

She fell into step beside him, easily keeping pace with his long strides, even though she was nearly a head shorter than he.

She waited until they were nearly to the trees, a small orchard of chestnut trees, before she spoke softly. "I thank you for the rescue, Mr. Gardiner."

"I cannot accept your thanks for that. I think your need for rescue was my fault." He directed her to a path between the trees, leading to the edge of the forest upon the duke's lands. "The moment I sat down, the ladies began sharpening their knives."

"Not Lady Josephine. Nor Miss Arlen," she corrected him, that near-smile appearing again as she puffed out a laugh. "But yes, I do believe Miss Finchley and either Miss Hapsworth would happily set their caps for you."

Her open assessment surprised a laugh from Rupert. "There now, Miss Sharpe. Didn't that feel wonderful to say?"

She laughed again, with more energy, and it faded away to reveal the same wide smile he had seen the first time they met. Before she knew he wasn't a gardener in the duke's employment.

Rupert relaxed at once, relieved beyond words that she had become comfortable around him once more. When she let her guard down, their conversation always proved much more enlightening. And diverting.

"Do you really have a flower to show me, Mr. Gardiner, or was it all a ruse to make sure my escape?" she asked, those lovely blue eyes twinkling at him.

Rupert's heart hummed in an approximation of the sound of a bee, happily at work at a flower.

He cleared his throat. "Actually, I wonder if you might like to see the bees I found yesterday. His Grace's beekeeper intends to tempt them with a hive this afternoon, so this will be my last chance to study them as they swarm."

Her fingers went to her throat. "Do we need to wear any netting?"

A practical question rather than a fearful one.

"We will not disturb them, only view their actions from afar." His free hand reached out, grasping her elbow for a moment in reassurance.

Miss Sharpe was an absolute marvel, and when she looked up at him with her confident smile and dancing eyes, Rupert found himself entirely entranced.

"Lead the way, Mr. Gardiner." She nodded to the forest. "I trust you to keep me safe."

ALICE FOLLOWED MR. GARDINER THROUGH THE STAND OF chestnut trees, around an open field, and to the edge of the forest. The closer the trees loomed, the closer she drew to the gentleman's side. She had no love for the closed-in woods and had not since becoming lost in a similar forest near her great-uncle's home.

Thankfully, Mr. Gardiner stopped several feet from the first tree with its gnarled, grasping branches.

"Here. Stand quiet and still. You will hear them." He put down his things, and Alice lowered his net to the pile he made. Then she held her sketchbook to her chest and listened.

At first she heard nothing but the wind and the rustle of the grass.

Then she heard the heavy buzz of hundreds of bees. Narrowing her eyes, she searched the tree line until she saw them, darting above the branches, flying in tight circles around one another. Her mouth fell open. "They sound as though they are rather angry. Are you certain it is safe to be this close?"

Mr. Gardiner moved closer, their shoulders nearly brushing, as he gazed in the same direction she did. "Quite certain. Yesterday, I stood directly beneath them and they paid me no heed." He sighed rather deeply. "The beekeeper hasn't the first idea where they are from. No one has reported their bees missing, he said. So these are likely wild, hunting for a place to begin a new colony with a young queen."

Alice looked up again, the bonnet shading her eyes from the afternoon sun. "It is an impressive sight. How will the beekeeper capture them?"

"Mr. Badger—that is his proper name, you needn't raise your eyebrows at me like that—will bring an empty hive-box beneath the tree. He will bait it with honeycomb from another hive. If they come inside and find they like it, they do most of his work for him. He need only wait until dusk to put them to sleep with a little smoke, then he can carry them back to where the rest of His Grace's bees are kept."

The process fascinated Alice, and Mr. Gardiner obviously took a great interest in it. "I did not even know the duke kept bees until today."

"Most grand houses keep their own bees, unless there is an accomplished beekeeper nearby to do the task." Mr. Gardiner shifted his stance, turning more toward her. His hand found her elbow again, touching her lightly. "I know you have your own work to see to today, Miss Sharpe, but I wanted to ask if I might send you more flowers to study. A third grouping. I planned to gather them today." He gestured to the basket on the ground.

"Oh. Of course." Alice tried to ignore his hand, alarmed as she was by her awareness of exactly where his fingertips lingered.

Despite his glove, despite her long-sleeved gown, heat simmered there upon her skin and crept throughout the rest of her.

"Thank you." His hand fell back to his side, and his gaze lowered to the ground. "I meant what I said before."

Alice studied the line of his jaw, the way his eyebrows pulled together far too seriously. "What you said before?" she repeated, trying to calm her racing pulse.

"To the ladies. You have a wonderful gift, Miss Sharpe, and I am grateful for it. You have lifted part of the burden from my shoulders. I only wish I knew how to thank you properly." He raised those dark eyes, meeting her stare squarely. Catching her studying him.

Alice's mouth dried and her throat momentarily closed, and all thought fled as his gaze captured hers.

When had anyone given her such undivided attention? She could not recall a time when someone looked at her as though she meant something to them, as though she were important in her own right.

"You have already thanked me, when I was less than gracious about the responsibility." She was nearly ashamed to admit as much, though logically she still knew she had been justified in her frustration with him.

Somehow, it no longer mattered that she must give up her own time for his project.

His expression softened, the look in his eyes gentle and almost admiring. He tilted his head closer, and Alice realized she had begun to lean toward him.

Abruptly she stepped back, raising her sketchbook higher as though it could shield her from—from whatever it was that had almost happened.

"Tomorrow is my half day, after the children have breakfast," she blurted. "I can work more upon the illustrations then."

Mr. Gardiner's expression changed to bemusement, then slowly he shook his head. "I cannot allow that, Miss Sharpe. You must have some time for yourself. Even I must take breaks from this work, to clear my mind and let it rest. When one works until they are overtired of a subject, they are more likely to make mistakes."

He turned back to studying the swarming bees at the edge of the wood. He crossed his arms over his chest and relaxed.

"But I could spend the entire day on your sketches," Alice protested, canting her head to the side. "I might accomplish much without interruption."

Mr. Gardiner chuckled, still facing the trees.

"Absolutely not. I will not hear of it." He spoke with a friendliness she had not expected, despite issuing his suggestion as a command. "Come now, Miss Sharpe. There must be something else you would rather do. What plans did you have for your half days before I appeared, confounding you and claiming all your free moments for my own?"

Alice considered the question, sorting through her thoughts and trying to remember if she had ever had any plans. A short walk would take her to the village supporting Castle Clairvoir. Lambsthorpe's main street boasted little more than a grocer and millinery, with a public house and inn should she wish to find a bite of food.

Then she looked back the way they had come, knowing the gardens would be overrun if the next day proved pleasant. That left her with little to do outside of the castle.

Perhaps she might enter the library—but then, since the duke and duchess had guests, she might be unwanted in the public rooms.

When she peered up at Mr. Gardiner again, and somewhat sheepishly lifted one shoulder in a shrug, she had to admit the truth of her situation. "I honestly cannot think of another way to spend my time. Perhaps reading. Or preparing lessons for the coming week."

His eyes stayed upon the trees and bees, and the muscles of

his jaw worked a moment before he spoke in a way that sounded off-hand.

"Perhaps you might spend part of your time with me." He still did not look at her as he extended the invitation. "You might tell me more about your interest in flora. Or we might walk through the statue gardens—you were in such a hurry that first time, you may have missed some things."

Could she believe her own ears? Had Mr. Gardiner, a gentleman and guest to the Duke of Montfort, invited her on an unchaperoned outing?

Of course, as a governess, no one really expected her to ever need a chaperone.

But no one expected a governess to be courted.

Was he attempting to court her?

No, of course not. She was merely overthinking things.

But what if—?

She had waited too long to speak, as his reddening cheeks accompanied his next words.

"If you would rather not, I understand—"

She hastened to interrupt him before she quite knew what she was doing. "I would be delighted, Mr. Gardiner. What time would you like to meet for a walk?"

Finally he turned to face her, a smile upon his face which lit up his entire countenance. He rubbed the back of his neck with one hand, arching an eyebrow at her. "If it is agreeable to you, perhaps we might meet before tea? I may be able to procure us something from the kitchens, to further enjoy the afternoon."

Her heartbeat sped up rather alarmingly. "That is most agree-able." Oh dear. Those words came out more breathless than she expected. "Two o'clock, then?"

"Yes. That will do nicely."

At that time of day, most of the ladies would likely retire to their rooms to rest before the evening meal. Children would be forced into quieter indoor activities to keep them out of the heat of the day, too. No one would see them, which meant no one would gossip about why a gentleman and a governess wandered through the gardens together.

Alice had to force away her own delighted smile. "Wonderful. I look forward to it. But for now, I must go. I have left my charges in the care of others too long."

"Of course." He bowed but kept his gaze upon her. "Until tomorrow."

"Tomorrow," she repeated with her curtsy. Then she hurried away, only glancing back once she was safely beneath the chestnut trees.

Mr. Gardiner watched and raised his hand in a final wave.

Alice hoped her blush had faded when she reached the meadow, even though her grin was far more difficult to hide.

CHAPTER 12

"Billings!" Rupert crawled on his hands and knees beneath his bed, searching for his missing boots. "Where are my Hessians?"

His valet cleared his throat loudly enough that Rupert sat up to glare at him, only to see both boots in the man's grasp.

"Oh."

"Yes, sir." Billings lowered the boots and glanced over Rupert's hasty efforts to dress himself. "Might I inquire as to the occasion for changing your clothes from what you decided upon this morning?" The valet cast a meaningful glance at the coat and cravat already discarded over the desk.

Rupert stood, trying to appear as though crawling about in his room was quite normal. "Ah. That. Well. This morning I was working in the gardens."

Billings arched an eyebrow. "Yes, sir."

"And this afternoon—I am not."

"You are not." Billings appeared somewhat concerned.

"Not working in the gardens." Rupert touched the knotted cravat somewhat self-consciously. "Would you fix this dashed piece of sailcloth?"

Billings put the boots upon the ground, carefully standing them up to avoid creasing the leather, then came to the rescue of Rupert's half-strangled throat. "Sir, your neckcloths are always of the finest linen. To imply that I would procure anything but the best for your use is somewhat insulting."

His valet's dry sense of humor had always amused Rupert more than louder sorts of jests. It also put him at ease. His valet was not put out with him. "I am aware of your efforts to make me appear presentable, and I thank you for them. I suppose I am something of a trial for you."

"Not at all, sir." The valet removed the crumpled cloth and went in search of a fresh strip of white linen. "You intend to be out of doors this afternoon, but not working." It was an observation, but Rupert recognized the question, too. Hessians were not appropriate footwear to wander about a castle. But they were acceptable for riding or the outdoors.

The only reason to hide what Rupert was about would be his own uncertainty. The exposure of his plans to another might cause future embarrassment if they came to naught.

Rupert cast a glance at the shelves against the wall without books or baubles, instead full of his cages of specimens. A cricket chirped, the sound calming to Rupert's tightened nerves. He turned back to his valet and tried to smile.

"I am meeting Miss Sharpe for a walk in the gardens." The admission, once made, caused his chest to tighten. What if she did not come? What if she came only to avoid offering him insult? Or what if they had nothing to say to one another once together?

Somewhat impossibly, Billings changed posture. His shoulders squared, his chin lifted, and a knowing gleam appeared in his eyes. "Miss Sharpe. Of course. Here, sir. Not the blue coat, the green. And you mustn't wear the broad-brimmed hat. Something more elegant—ah, the brown beaver. It lends height to your stature." The valet went about the room like a whirlwind caught indoors, but with efficiency rather than destruction.

Rupert watched in some confusion but obeyed when Billings instructed him to hold out arms for his coat and lift his chin for a fresh cravat. Then Billings forced Rupert into a chair in order to fuss with his hair. After lamenting the lack of time for a trim, Billings took up the Hessians and shoved them—without ceremony—onto Rupert's feet.

"What else do you need, sir?" Billings asked, eyeing Rupert's clothing critically.

"I thought I would go to the kitchens for a basket?" Rupert did not mean to make the statement into a question, but given the valet's reaction to Rupert's plans, he found himself rather uncertain.

"An excellent idea. I will go for you, and I will leave the basket somewhere in the gardens. You have no wish to carry the thing everywhere with you. What would be the most convenient location?"

The valet had a point. Rupert laughed, rubbing the back of his neck. "I had thought to tour the statue garden with Miss Sharpe."

"Excellent. I will leave the basket at the foot of Apollo."

Rupert raised his eyebrows. "You know the gardens?"

"Of course, sir. I enjoy a turn out of doors on occasion." Billings smiled, almost secretively. Perhaps he had escorted his own fair guest through the gardens. Though the idea of his valet offering courtship to any young lady proved hard to picture.

"I will see to the basket at once," Billings said, standing back to take in Rupert's appearance one more time. "There you are, sir. I will clean up this mess after I have settled matters with the basket." He gestured to the disorder in the room. "Good luck to you, Mr. Gardiner." Then he vanished out the door with only the slightest, most hurried of bows.

Rupert turned to the mirror hanging above the chest of drawers, then grinned to himself. "I think Billings approves of Miss Sharpe."

For some reason, that made his heart lighter. Perhaps he was not such a fool in seeking out her company.

DESPITE HER INITIAL MISGIVINGS—MR. GARDINER COULD not really wish to spend his time with *her,* could he?—excitement rose in Alice's breast with each passing hour of the morning. She sat in the schoolroom with the other governesses and children, a book open in her lap. But she could not concentrate enough to read more than a single line without drifting away in thought.

"I cannot believe they give you your half-day even when the family has guests." Miss Felton had proven sourer by the day, especially after Alice and Mr. Gardiner had taken charge of young Geoffrey. "One would think your duty to the family more important than wasting time."

Even Miss Felton's horrid disposition would not quell Alice's anxious happiness. She gifted the woman a smile. "I am most fortunate that Her Grace insists upon her staff being well rested, so that we may serve her and the family better."

"It is not as if we are infants," Lady Isabelle added from where she sat at the school table, picking at a sampler.

Color appeared in Miss Felton's cheeks. "Of course not, my lady. I am certain you are quite a capable girl."

Lady Rosalind looked up from the game she played with one of the other guests. "Truly, Miss Sharpe deserves a little time to herself. She is our favorite of all the governesses we have had."

The defense from her charges both surprised and gratified Alice. She tried to hide her smile but made certain to offer them a wink when they looked her way. Treating the girls as ladies, capable of thought as well as choosing their own interests, had apparently endeared them to her.

Lord James was another story. He was across the room, doing sums with two other boys under the direction of their governess.

Alice had no doubt he would get into some sort of mischief the moment they left him unsupervised. He still had not quite forgiven her for removing the frogs from his room, though he had seemed to understand the need for it.

Alice turned a page, then checked the watch she had hidden in her lap beneath the book's cover. Her half-day had begun.

Closing the book, and pinning the watch to her bodice, she went to stand between Lady Isabelle and Lady Rosalind. "I am going to my room now. I trust you two will look after things."

"Miss Sharpe, Isabelle and I wondered if we might speak to you in private for a moment?" Lady Rosalind stood, casting a glance to her elder sister.

Isabelle stood, too, dropping her embroidery into her empty chair. "Yes, please. We have something of great importance to discuss with you. In private."

Startled, Alice could only nod and gesture to the door. "Of course. Accompany me to my room. We may speak there."

The sisters followed her out the door and down the narrow corridor to her room. She allowed them to step inside first before entering and closing the door behind her. They both looked around with curiosity for a moment, Isabelle deciding to sit upon the bed while Rosalind took the only available chair.

They both fixed Alice with serious stares.

Her excitement ebbed away, replaced with concern for the girls. "Dear me. Whatever is the matter? I have never seen you both appear so solemn. Have I done something wrong?"

"Not at all," Isabelle said, exchanging a look with her sister. "But we heard Josephine and Emma talking about yesterday. When Mr. Gardiner took you away."

Alice's cheeks immediately gave her away, heating up like bricks tucked into embers. "Oh—he only wished to show me the bees. And flowers. So I might better assist him."

"That isn't what Josephine said," Rosalind announced, her smile appearing. "Josephine said he practically rescued you from the others, and you were gone for more than a quarter of an hour, and that when you came back you could not stop smiling."

"Emma thinks you like him," Isabelle added, a triumphant gleam in her eye. "I think she's right."

Knowing that the duke's eldest daughter and her companion had discussed Alice in such a way, and before the younger girls, made her feel ill at ease. "I—I do not mean to act in a way contrary to what is expected. I know my first duty is to my position as governess. I would never dream—"

Lady Isabelle laughed. "Miss Sharpe, you needn't worry. *We* do not disapprove."

But their mother might. If word of Alice's time spent with Mr. Gardiner reached the duchess, if she found out there was more to their time together than the duke's project, Alice's position might well be in peril.

"Are you going to see Mr. Gardiner today?" Lady Rosalind asked, sitting on the edge of her chair. "What are you going to wear? Mama says a woman's choice of gown is as much about communicating what a lady thinks of her company as it is about looking her best."

Alice put her hand to her throat, considering the question while trying to brush away the unease the girls had caused. "I—I thought I would wear this." She lowered her hand to run it down the front of her dark brown, serviceable gown. The long sleeves might be impractical for a summer day, but they would protect her skin from the sun.

Identical looks of horror appeared on the girls' faces.

"*No,* Miss Sharpe!" Lady Isabelle shook her head adamantly.

"You cannot keep a tryst wearing *that*," the more romantically minded Lady Rosalind said sharply.

Alice felt her cheeks warm. "It is *not* a tryst."

They both raised their eyebrows, then Lady Isabelle hopped to her feet. "Regardless, we cannot let you go for a walk with a gentleman wearing *that*. It's all well and good to look frumpy in the schoolroom—"

"Frumpy?" Alice nearly laughed.

"—but you cannot stroll through a beautiful garden in a gown the color of mud," Lady Isabelle finished severely, sounding older than her fourteen years. "What else do you have?" She went to the small wardrobe in the corner. "There must be something more suitable."

Lady Rosalind stood, too. "And we must do something with your hair. Must you always wear it in such a severe knot?"

"It is hardly the concern of a governess to look attractive," Alice argued, somewhat weakly.

"Nonsense. You are barely older than Josephine, but you dress like that horrid Miss Felton." Rosalind sniffed, then pulled the chair to the middle of the room. "Sit. We will help you."

Alice's protests went unheard as the duke's daughters took out every dress she owned— only six, at present—and cast each one upon the bed. Blue, gray, and brown day dresses were pronounced too matronly. The lilac evening gown met with wrinkled noses. The last two gowns apparently merited some study, however.

Lady Rosalind held one up to Alice's chin. The gown was a pale blue, matching Alice's eyes. It had been a gift from the same great-aunt who recommended her for the position of governess. The sleeves were long, the neckline high and modest, but the cut of the bodice *did* flatter Alice. The color made her eyes stand out, even from behind the clear lenses of her spectacles.

"That is pretty," Lady Isabelle said. "What about the other one?"

Lady Rosalind put the other gown, a peach-colored dress with tiny rosettes at the sleeves, to Alice's shoulders. The gown had been gifted to her by another relative, a cousin who had worn it only once and decided it did not suit her. Alice had worn it to church when there were weddings after the Sabbath services.

The elder sister cooed like a dove. "Oh, it's lovely. Perfect for today. I think we ought to save the blue one for another outing."

"Another outing?" Alice said, somewhat weakly. Would there be more somewhat clandestine meetings with Mr. Gardiner?

She found she rather hoped so.

"I agree," Lady Rosalind said. "Put this on, Miss Sharpe, and then we will fix your hair."

Alice did not know whether to be grateful or annoyed that girls so much younger than her had taken it upon themselves to prepare her for her meeting with Mr. Gardiner.

Gratitude soon won out, however, as her charges showered compliments upon her head. When they stood back to observe their handiwork, Alice's heart lightened upon the pronouncement that she was very pretty.

"If only we could do away with the spectacles," Lady Isabelle said.

"Oh, they are not so bad." Lady Rosalind narrowed her eyes. "They make you look very scholarly, Miss Sharpe."

Rather than admit she did not need them *all* the time, Alice simply adjusted the spectacles on her nose. "I cannot think what good removing them would actually do."

"Merely allow your eyes to show off to a better advantage," Lady Isabelle answered with a single shoulder shrug. "But if you had to go about squinting, that would be worse. I think we have framed your face with your curls quite prettily."

"I think Mr. Gardiner will be surprised. If he liked you before, he can only think you even prettier today." Lady Rosalind sighed happily.

Alice looked into her small, square mirror. "Quite right, Lady Rosalind. Although—although I must protest again. Mr. Gardiner is not—he cannot be interested in me as anything other than a temporary colleague."

She caught the skeptical raise of Lady Isabelle's eyebrows in the mirror. "If you say so, Miss Sharpe."

A warm, comfortable feeling settled in Alice's heart, at odds with the way her stomach had twisted and turned before. To have such fine young ladies show so much interest in her, a nobody and their governess besides, gave her greater confidence. She checked her watch.

It was a quarter 'til two o'clock and time to meet Mr. Gardiner in the statue gardens. She took in a deep breath and reached for her bonnet.

CHAPTER 13

R upert paced at the break in the roses that led from the upper terrace down into the statue gardens. He kept checking his pocket watch, though he had arrived early.

What if she did not come? What if she had decided against spending the hours of her freedom with him? Or what if she had questioned the propriety of their meeting and decided against the risk to her reputation?

Though most considered governesses both beneath their notice and above reproach, Miss Sharpe had made it clear how aware she was of her status in the household. If she cast aside his reassurances, the fear for her position might well keep her away.

What a shame that would be.

At five minutes until two o'clock, Rupert stuffed his watch into his waistcoat pocket. He tried to turn his attention to a moth resting on one of the roses, noting how its behavior differed from a butterfly a few roses over. The markings on the dark brown moth put him in mind of tree bark, which made the creature stand out while it rested on the pink petals of the flower. Yet it appeared safe from predators, since it resembled flora rather than fauna.

The crunch of a step on the gravel brought Rupert's attention back to the path, and his heart sprang into his throat the way a cricket might jump through the grass. He turned his gaze to the archway at the moment Miss Sharpe stepped into it, her expression uncertain, her smile slight. Her visage—beautiful.

The color of her gown put him in mind of the clouded yellow butterfly's wingtips—a delicate shade which emphasized her natural coloring prettily. Her blush upon catching his stare was nearly the same shade, and all at once Rupert wanted to take her in his arms and offer her shelter.

His mouth went dry, and his throat tightened. His words came out somewhat strangled. "Miss Sharpe. You came."

She placed a gloved hand to her throat and looked down. "As I said I would, Mr. Gardiner."

"Rupert."

Her gaze rose, her lips parted in surprise. "Rupert?" Had anything ever sounded so right as his name falling from her tongue?

"My Christian name." His stomach knotted and he tried to laugh. He had forgotten to think before speaking. His complete lack of decorum would endanger the whole afternoon. He tried to offer up excuses, poorly constructed as they were. "We are friends, are we not? But if you prefer, you might call me Gardiner instead. Unless you are uncomfortable with the whole idea, in which case, I must apologize—"

"Rupert," she said again, more firmly. "It is a fine name. You must call me Alice." Her cheeks remained that lovely pink shade, despite the sudden determination in her eyes. "We are friends, as you say. And colleagues. But perhaps—we should only do so in private—?"

"Of course," he agreed hastily, stepping closer and offering her his hand. "That would be best, I agree. I am glad to see you." When she gave him her hand, he bowed over it. "Alice."

She could not know what a gift her name was to him. Or that

he decided, in that instant, if he ever discovered a new species of butterfly, he meant to name it after her.

Then he tucked her hand into the crook of his arm. "Where should we begin our tour? I have refreshments waiting for us at Apollo."

"I think at whichever statue is closest. I hurried by most of them before." She tipped her head to the side, allowing him a clearer view of her profile. "As you might recall, I was not paying a great deal of attention to my surroundings at the time."

"Ah, yes. You did become rather closely acquainted with a flowerbed." He chuckled at the memory. Had it only been a fortnight since they met? It felt as though he knew her longer. Perhaps the amount of time she had taken up his thoughts made it so.

They walked along the path, pausing at each statue as they went. Alice—how he enjoyed the use of her Christian name—knew each statue's identity with only the barest hints in the sculptures. She was well-versed in mythology, a subject he did not think most women knew.

Then he would point out the plants growing around each statue, telling her more about them, and noting when they flowered or slept for a season. Not once did she seem impatient or uninterested at his explanations. Alice listened, her eyes upon him, asking intelligent questions from time to time.

When they arrived at Apollo, within sight of the statue of Aphrodite, Rupert scooped up the basket at the base of the Greek god. He would have to thank Billings profusely for the man's foresight. "Why don't we venture over there?" he asked, pointing to the statue of the goddess where they had first met. "I understand there is a well-tended bed of narcissus."

Alice's laugh danced through the air between them. "I suppose that would be appropriate, given it was the scene of our first meeting. You were rather impatient with me, you will recall."

"And you were certain I was concerned about the flowers you crushed." He followed after her, admiring the grace of her walk.

"I thought you were a gardener," she reminded him over her shoulder.

Rupert bit back a sigh of admiration. He had to get hold of himself. He had been around many a beautiful woman before. Had both charmed ladies and repelled them, at his choice, with either mild flirtation or stories about his insect collection. All his interactions with Alice Sharpe, however, had been different. She seemed charmed by his talk of crawling things and repelled by his attempts at flirting—at least at first. Things were markedly different now. Her reactions sent his head spinning, and their time together was never quite enough for him to determine what it was that drew him to her.

They settled beneath the statue, on a blanket Billings had thoughtfully added to the basket. Rupert served her a cup of lemonade from a small jug, then fruit and cheese.

"How did you become a governess, Alice?" he asked after he had settled in with his own refreshment. "You talked of your family before, when we tended to Geoffrey. Why are you not with them?"

Her eyes lowered to the flowers, and one hand idly plucked grapes from their stem. "My parents died when I was very young. I cannot remember my father at all, though I do remember my mother. We lived with one of her sisters for a time, before she fell ill and died. My aunt kept me for a few years, but she had several of her own children to occupy her time. I was sent to my father's mother. Then she passed away, and I went to an uncle. Then another aunt, and then everyone blurs together."

She had been like Geoffrey, passed from one guardian to another. Never quite settling, never belonging.

"My great-aunt, Mrs. Lucinda Beardsley, was the last person I was with. I acted as her companion for a time, but then she was summoned to help one of her granddaughters enter Society. That was when the family decided I ought to try for more independence."

Though Alice spoke calmly, her words practiced and clearly carefully measured, something about her story struck him as terribly sad. Lonely, even.

"You became a governess."

She plucked another grape but left it on the plate rather than sample it. "To the duke's family. Yes. My great-aunt recommended me to the dowager duchess."

"This is your first position?" Rupert sat back on his hands, considering her reluctance to help him with his work. It made more sense that she would worry so, given that her family had sent her away with such heavy expectations upon her shoulders.

Alice shrugged. "My very first, officially, though I have acted as a tutor for many of my younger cousins. I am quite familiar with children and schoolrooms. I have always tried to make myself useful."

The smallness of her voice at that admission caused his heart to crack. How could anyone make her feel of such little value that she had to make herself *useful* to live with her own family? No wonder she kept quiet in the presence of others. No wonder she defended the orphaned Geoffrey with such kindness. How little of that had she known in her own youth, passed from one household to another?

Rupert put aside his plate and reached for her hand before she could tug another grape off the stem only to let it roll freely about her plate. She looked up at him, startled, as he drew her hand close to his heart. Fixing her with what he hoped was a reassuring smile, Rupert spoke earnestly.

"Everything I know about you, Alice Sharpe, speaks of your intelligence, warmth, and kindness. You are quick-witted and a true pleasure to be near. I value our friendship, though it is early days yet. I am most grateful to have your help with my work, and I cannot imagine how anyone could see you as anything less than a lady of quality."

Her lips parted, and her eyebrows raised high, but no word

escaped her. Not for a long moment, as she seemed to evaluate his words and the truth behind them. At last she smiled, her expression softening in a way that made him want to draw closer, though he resisted the urge.

"Thank you, Rupert. That is one of the kindest things anyone has ever said to me."

He gave her hand a gentle squeeze before lowering it, ignoring the desire to pull her into a most improper embrace. He had only just gained her trust and friendship. He would not lose it merely to give way to his impulses.

He had never met a woman like her. And he very much wanted to know more, know *everything*, about Alice.

But she had a position to protect, and he would not do anything to alarm her.

He needed to take things slow.

With great reluctance, he began to clear away their picnic and turned the conversation back to flowers and bees.

ALICE FLOATED BACK INTO THE HOUSE, UP THE SERVANTS' stairs, and to her room. Once there, she closed the door behind her and leaned heavily against it. Never in her life had someone paid such pointed attention to her. Not once in her memory had a man looked upon her as though she were more than a curiosity.

Her family had hinted that she held attraction for the opposite sex, and they had even deemed her a danger to her own daughters due to that fact. But Alice had thought them wrong, or else mistaken in their assessment of her looks.

For the first time, in Rupert Gardiner's company, she had felt *beautiful*.

Alice went to her desk as she removed her gloves, humming to herself, when she saw a slip of paper that had not been there before. Frowning, she lifted it and turned it over to reveal a note.

The Duke and Duchess have decided to allow the children to perform this evening, with instruments and recitations. Before they take dinner with their guests, at five o'clock sharp. You are to prepare the duke's children. - F.

With less than two hours to prepare herself and her charges, Alice leaped into movement. She took off her peach dress and pulled on the dark blue gown still laying across her bed from when Lady Isabelle had discarded it. She did up the front buttons, grateful for the practical gown, but she had no time to fix her hair.

She flew out of her room in search of the girls and Lord James. She had to ensure their appropriate dress for the evening and help them choose either a piece to play or a poem to recite that would gratify their parents' guests.

If only she'd had more notice. If only they had more time to prepare.

Would a poor showing of the children mean a reprimand for her?

She started with Lord James, certain he would be the most difficult of the three to prepare. She knocked upon his door in the children's part of the hall, and it opened to reveal him and several of the other boys playing at soldiers on the floor of his room.

"Lord James, you must dress for dinner this evening. There is—"

"A performance," he said, interrupting her. His wide grin kept her from feeling any offense. "Josephine told us. I'm to go last. Want to hear my recitation?"

Alice raised her eyebrows and folded her hands before her. "You already have something prepared?"

"Yes. I thought I could give Puck's speech from the end of the play we read last week."

"From *A Midsummer Night's Dream?*" Alice gaped at him. "Lord James, that would be perfect. I had nearly forgotten you memorized it." Indeed, he had focused so much of his attention on frogs and catapults of late, his other activities had nearly eclipsed his interest in the mischievous Puck.

What better way to end an evening of children's displays than Puck's monologue?

"Did Lady Josephine inform your sisters, too?"

The boy nodded. "They're getting dressed right now." He wrinkled his nose. "Why do girls take so long to get dressed?"

Alice laughed as the last of her nerves dissipated. "It is a mystery, my lord. One you may never untangle. But do lay out your own suit of clothing, so I may check it over, please."

"Yes, Miss Sharpe." He looked over his shoulder. "Come on, fellows. We had better turn ourselves out." He flashed his grin at Alice. "We'll be ready soon." Then he closed the door.

Alice stepped backward until she leaned against the wall. It seemed she owed Lady Josephine her gratitude. Then she straightened and went to the room shared by Lady Isabelle and Lady Rosalind. She would assist them however she could and ensure neither of them suffered from nerves over their upcoming performance.

CHAPTER 14

Billings did not ask any questions as he helped Rupert dress once more, this time for the children's recital and the evening meal. But Rupert sensed his valet's curiosity enough that it amused him to keep silent about his afternoon with Alice.

Warmth spread through his chest even thinking her name. He had her friendship, which brought about a great deal of satisfaction, but he dearly wanted *more*.

Thankfully, he had the entire summer to work upon gaining her affection. Despite their relatively brief acquaintance, he knew she was special. He could feel it in his heart and soul.

As his valet put the last touch in place, a sapphire stickpin in Rupert's cravat, he at last broke his silence with his sincere gratitude. "Thank you for your help, Billings. The basket you provided for my walk with Miss Sharpe was excellent."

The valet relaxed and stepped back, a smile briefly appearing upon his stoic face. "I am pleased I could be of assistance, sir."

Rupert took the conversation a step further. "I take it you approve of Miss Sharpe."

Billings appeared thoughtful as he answered. "I approve of anyone who esteems you and your work, sir."

With a nod, Rupert surveyed himself one last time in the mirror. "Thank you, Billings. That will do. I doubt I will need anything else this evening. You may spend your time as you will."

The valet nodded. "Very good, sir. Thank you."

Rupert left the room in high spirits. Word of the children's performance had reached him, and he had a feeling he would catch another glimpse of Alice that evening because of it.

He made his way to the music room, and when he entered saw that chairs were filled both with children and their parents alike. The doors to the next room over, a study, were open to allow for more seating. The duke and duchess had added local neighbors to the guest list for the evening.

He found the duke's three youngest children with his gaze; they sat in the front row of chairs with their parents and eldest sister. But where, then, would Alice sit? It took him a moment to find her, seated beside three other women dressed in dark clothing. He recognized the governess, Miss Felton, sitting with her customary scowl in place. Alice, sitting beside her in a gown of deep blue, appeared all the lovelier with her contrasting expression of anticipation.

She caught sight of him at nearly the same moment, and he had the pleasure of watching her smile before she offered the smallest of waves. Rupert inclined his head toward her, then found a seat among the guests.

If only they had met before she became a governess. Then there would be little to keep him from seeking her out among company.

Lady Josephine stood after the room had filled, apparently taking on the role of hostess for the evening. She thanked everyone for coming and introduced the first several children who would perform. Rupert sat back in his chair, crossing his arms. His gaze kept drifting to Alice, but every time, he found her watching the children with rapt attention.

Some of the performances were quite good. The only uncomfortable portion of the evening occurred when one of the baron's sons attempted to play a complicated piece on the violin.

Dying cats sounded more musical than the screech of the boy's bow across the strings. Yet the audience applauded enthusiastically at his attempts.

When Lady Rosalind and Lady Isabelle played a duet of some complexity, Rupert covertly watched as Alice beamed with true pleasure at their talent.

Then Lord James stood and began his monolog.

"If we shadows have offended,
Think but this, and all is mended,
That you have but slumber'd here
While these visions did appear.
And this weak and idle theme,
No more yielding but a dream,
Gentles, do not reprehend:
if you pardon, we will mend:
And, as I am an honest Puck,
If we have unearned luck
Now to 'scape the serpent's tongue,
We will make amends ere long;
Else the Puck a liar call;
So, good night unto you all.
Give me your hands, if we be friends,
And Robin shall restore amends."

No child could have done Puck as much justice as Lord James, keeping mischief in his eyes the entire recitation, then looking to his ducal father with bright and hopeful eyes.

The duke applauded with the rest of the company assembled, then stood while still clapping his hands for the performance of all the children. The room followed suit, as all the young performers beamed at one another.

As the applause died away, His Grace turned to address the company.

In the quiet just before the duke spoke, a sudden, loud *croak* filled the silent air.

Everyone somehow became quieter still, but Rupert had to cover his mouth to avoid a laugh. The duke's gaze immediately fell to his son beside him, both his eyebrows raised. Rupert glanced at Alice—but rather than appear amused, her face was pale as milk.

"James," the duke said, his deep voice rolling over the company. "I think you had better release your prisoner before you make your way to bed."

The little boy squirmed and put a hand over his chest pocket, doubtless checking the movement of the frog. "Yes, Your Grace."

Then the duke chuckled and put his hand on the boy's shoulder. The whole room seemed to release a long-held breath. "My Puck. You did well tonight. As did all the children. Thank you, my young gentlemen and ladies both. You have done your parents great credit this evening. Good night to you all. May the nursery be filled with your peaceful slumber amid pleasant dreams."

That pronouncement gave the audience leave to mingle with the children, offering compliments and good nights.

As people rose from their chairs, Rupert hurried to where the governesses stood, quietly waiting for the moment to take their charges in hand once more.

Rupert bowed to Alice the moment he drew near enough. "Miss Sharpe, I must say that your students performed beautifully."

She blushed and offered him her curtsy. "Thank you, Mr. Gardiner. It was a joy to watch them. As I have only been with the family a fortnight, I cannot take any credit."

"But some of the blame for that frog," Miss Felton muttered to the other governesses, loud enough for Rupert and Alice to hear. The other educators covered their mouths and snickered.

Alice's cheeks pinked.

Rupert's ire rose, along with a wicked desire to make the ladies uncomfortable as they had done to Alice. "Lord James has shown a great interest in animals this summer. Why, only last month, he had a tame rat he brought about everywhere with him."

Miss Felton's bushy eyebrows rose. "A rat?"

"Yes. I understand he left it in the last governess's chambers when she proved unpleasant." He smiled, likely a little too innocently. "His little pets are usually the means of his childish revenge. He has been trying to catch spiders, too. I think he has some wish to see what would happen if he released them amid company such as this."

Miss Felton and the other governesses appeared rather horrified.

"I have half a mind to help him," Rupert added.

"Mr. Gardiner," Alice said suddenly, stepping forward. "Perhaps you might assist Lord James in returning his frog outdoors, while I help the other children—our guests—to the nursery? He does admire you so."

Rupert raised his eyebrows at her, noting the somewhat anxious smile she wore. "Very well. After that, I will see him safely returned to the children's wing."

"Thank you, sir." As she stepped around him, between the other governesses and he, she lightly touched his hand and he caught one corner of her mouth creeping upward in a smile.

Rather than watch her go, he searched out Lord James. The duke was speaking to his son in a quiet, stern voice.

"—after the incident with the other frogs, I thought you knew better than to bring more of the creatures indoors."

"But this isn't a frog, Papa," the boy said quietly, expression earnest. "It is a toad."

The duke appeared momentarily surprised, then he covered a grin with his hand. "Regardless, your animal needs to be outside where it belongs, James. They are not meant to live indoors any more than you are meant to live in a pond."

"Your Grace, Lord James." Rupert bowed to them both. "I

wonder if I might assist in returning the creature to its home. I should enjoy a little fresh air before dinner."

The duke turned to Rupert with a welcoming smile. "Ah, Gardiner. I am certain my son would appreciate your company."

Lord James nodded. "Yes, thank you, Mr. Gardiner."

"Before you go on your errand of mercy," the duke said, placing a hand on Rupert's shoulder. "You must tell me. Has Miss Sharpe proven an apt colorist? I meant to ask you last evening if you could bring me a sample of her work."

"As I have said before, Your Grace, she has a true talent. I am most grateful she has taken the time to help." Rupert gestured to Lord James. "I know she has used her personal hours to accomplish much, rather than allow her work as a governess to suffer. Tell me, Lord James, what do you think of Miss Sharpe as your governess?"

If he could do Alice a good turn, Rupert meant to do so. She deserved praise, and to be noticed, for her dedication to the duke's children.

Lord James did not disappoint him. "Miss Sharpe is the best governess we've had. She isn't dull at all, and she likes teaching us about things. She is letting me construct a trebuchet, but only after I can memorize King Henry's speech."

The duke appeared interested. "'Once more into the breech'?"

His son nodded. "That one. We're learning about the history of England. Miss Sharpe says Shakespeare didn't get all the facts right, so we're reading the play and history books at the same time. She lets me read Henry's parts."

"An intelligent approach to keep a boy's interest." The duke ruffled his son's hair. "It sounds as though you will be well prepared when it is time to go away to school."

Lord James grinned. "Yes, Papa."

"Off with you, now. Most of your friends have gone. Return the frog—pardon me. The toad." The duke shared an amused smile with Rupert. "I will see you at dinner shortly, Gardiner."

"Yes, Your Grace." Rupert bowed, then put his hand on Lord James's back and guided the boy out of the room.

"I'm sorry about the toad, Mr. Gardiner." Lord James put his hand over his coat again. "I didn't think he'd make such a loud noise."

Rupert chuckled. "It is evening, Lord James. Your toad is calling to his fellows, or to his lady."

The boy wrinkled his nose. "To his lady? Animals don't court, Mr. Gardiner."

"Who here is the naturalist?" Rupert led them down the stairs. "I assure you, they have their own forms of courtship. Some animals have even more complicated relationships than people."

After they released the toad in the kitchen gardens, where Rupert hoped it would prove useful, they went back up to the children's wing. They arrived to find the corridor empty except for Alice, patiently waiting for her last pupil's return. She offered the boy a warm smile that Rupert hoped extended to him, too.

"Lord James. Do you need anything before bed?"

"No, thank you." He bowed to her. "Good night, Miss Sharpe." Then he offered Rupert the same words of departure before slipping into his room.

Alice looked up at Rupert, her eyes shining with good humor. "That was quite an evening, wasn't it?" she asked, her voice low in the empty corridor.

"I enjoyed myself immensely." He could not help but stare at her, admiring everything from the blonde ringlet curled around her earlobe to a freckle on one cheek.

How had it happened that he, a man unconcerned with female beauty, could become an admirer of a woman with such speed? It was only natural, he supposed, that when a man found a woman of such talent and intelligence that he must find all aspects of her lovely and becoming.

She blushed beneath his gaze and took a single step back. "I must turn in as well. I have lessons to plan for tomorrow, and I should like to spend at least an hour on your sketches."

"I trust the flowers I sent found you well. I look forward to seeing your work again," he said. "If you think you have the time—"

"I do. The duke's guests leave after the ball in three days."

"The ball." He released a weary sigh. "I had forgotten about it again." Rupert ran a hand across his forehead and tried not to groan. "I detest balls. Making inane conversation with near strangers. Feigning interest in gowns and gossip."

She giggled at him. "I always enjoyed the dancing, though."

His hand fell away, and he caught the wistfulness of her smile. "I wish you could come." The words escaped before he could think them over.

Her expression grew more solemn, though her smile did not entirely vanish. "Governesses do not go to balls. But I have faith that you will do your best to make the time enjoyable for the other ladies present."

He did groan then, in an attempt to be comical and lighten the suddenly heavy air around them. "Must I, Alice? It does not seem fair, when I will spend the entire evening wishing I was studying wasps."

"You could always pretend the ladies are insects," she said, her playful smile returning. "You might spend the evening cataloging them and their behavior, all in the name of science."

Rupert chuckled and reached for her hand, quite without meaning to. "You might have something there." He closed his fingers around hers. "I told Lord James that toads have courtship rituals. Perhaps I will imagine all the ladies as toads."

"That would be excessively wicked of you." Alice looked down at their joined hands, not pulling away, but not offering any encouragement either. "You could at least think them something more pleasant. Rabbits, perhaps. Or hedgehogs."

He drew slightly nearer, studying her eyes beneath the glass of her spectacles. "And what classification would I put you beneath, Alice?"

Her gaze met his, and her lips parted. "I haven't any idea, sir. Something small. Inconsequential."

He shook his head, the movement slight. He leaned closer. "Never that. Perhaps the *Polyommatus coridon*. They are butterflies, with soft, white-tipped wings, though they are a bright blue at the center. They flutter above the low-growing flowers, bringing notice to themselves and the beauty people too often ignore."

She tipped her head upward, her lovely eyes studying his. "They sound enchanting."

"As are you, Alice."

Before he could breathe another word, a door down the hall clicked open.

Alice sprang backward, making him realize they had stood near enough to kiss.

He took a step back, too, before looking over his shoulder. It was Miss Felton, backing out of the room where her charges likely slept. She turned around and raised both eyebrows, seeing them together in the hall.

"Thank you for bringing Lord James back, Mr. Gardiner," Alice said, her voice firm and impersonal. "I hope you enjoy the rest of your evening."

Rupert turned his attention back to her and bowed. "Good evening, Miss Sharpe." Then he had no choice but to leave, nodding at Miss Felton as he went. He said nothing to her, and he schooled his features into the mask of a proper gentleman.

But for the rest of the evening, all he could do was debate whether or not it had been a good thing that someone had interrupted the moment between Alice and him.

Because he was fairly certain he had been about to kiss his beautiful blue butterfly...

CHAPTER 15

Alice didn't so much as glimpse Rupert for a week after the children's performance. He sent flowers, sketches, and an impersonal note wishing her well. She returned the sketches to his valet when she completed them.

The duke's guests left after the ball, which Alice heard about from Lady Josephine and Emma when they came for tea in the schoolroom.

They had both danced with Rupert, they informed her, and found superb entertainment when he told them he had been categorizing the ladies at the event into different insect families.

Otherwise, the routine went back to what it had been before the guests' arrival, but the reprieve was brief. June arrived, and with it more preparations for the duke to receive visitors.

"Simon is coming home," Lord James announced one morning after his return from his father's study. With the guests gone, the duke made time every morning for his youngest child. "Papa has had a letter from him, and he is bringing his friends."

Talk of the duke's eldest son returning home had come up nearly every day since Alice's arrival.

Lady Isabelle and Lady Rosalind exchanged enthusiastic smiles. "Simon's friends are *always* attractive," Lady Isabelle said.

"You are both far too young to worry over such things," Alice said without even looking up from her inspection of Lady Isabelle's drawing of a Spanish mosque. She had copied the building from a book on the subject of the Moors in Spain. Alice had hopes that Lady Isabelle's interest in religions would lead to some interest in architecture, or at least provide the girl with more understanding of the subject dear to her mother's heart.

Lady Rosalind emitted a dramatic sigh, putting her chin in her hand and her elbow upon the table. "*Someday* we must pay attention to gentlemen. We will have to marry. Eventually."

"Papa has said he will give us at least a little freedom to choose." Lady Isabelle fiddled with the pencil in her grasp, twisting and turning it. "I think I should study gentlemen now so I will know what I like before I am made to wed."

Alice looked up at the young woman. "Will your parents play a part in arranging your marriages?" She had not heard the girls speak of such a thing, though she knew that the highest ranks of the nobility were mostly populated through arrangement rather than affection.

"To an extent," Lady Isabelle answered with a shrug. "Josephine is expected to make an advantageous match before she is five and twenty."

"Oh." Given that Josephine was only eighteen years of age, that gave her lots of time to settle on her choice. "What constitutes an advantageous match for the daughters of a duke? One would think you outrank every gentleman in the kingdom, excepting any princes."

Lady Rosalind flipped a page in the book before her. "Money. Land. Any other title, I think, if Papa found the nobleman suitable."

Lady Isabelle nodded her agreement. "Especially if the man

was from another kingdom entirely. Papa is always saying that after the business with Napoleon that England must befriend more nations."

"I do suppose that all makes sense." Alice pointed to a spot on the sketch. "Here, I think you have curved this spire in too dramatically, Lady Isabelle."

The girl set about correcting the mistake without complaint. She intended to paint her drawing, guided only by description of the building in the text.

"I don't see why you are more excited about Simon's friends than the fact that *Simon* is coming home." Lord James dropped into a chair with a scowl. "We haven't seen him in an entire year."

The duke's eldest son and heir, holding the honorary title of the Earl of Farleigh, had been on a tour of Greece and Italy, from what Alice had gathered. He had visited Spain, France, and Prussia in the last year, too.

Lady Rosalind poked her younger brother with a finger. "Oh, hush. You know we are excited to see Simon. But we have had more than enough letters from him."

"You're only hoping he brings you presents," Lady Isabelle added with a knowing grin at her brother.

Lord James folded his arms. "I know he will, and you want presents as much as I do."

The girls laughed, but before they could tease their little brother into a foul mood, Alice pronounced a break in their work. "I think we ought to go for a walk in the gardens before dinner. I have had quite enough of this room for the day. Do you agree, children?"

Their response was immediate approval, and they all rushed from the room to gather hats and parasols, and whatever things they wished to bring to the gardens with them.

Alice tidied the things upon the table and left the rest of the room for the maids. The servants would not touch their school things but could be depended upon to set the rest of the room to rights before the next morning. That left Alice more time to see to her own tasks, thankfully.

She had been with the family for an entire month, and each day made her feel more at ease in her position. Never had she belonged in a place all her own, independent of her family's charity. Work was a far sight better than dependence.

Alice fixed her bonnet atop her head, tugged her gloves into place, and took her sketchbook with her to the corridor where the children waited. Lord James led the way down the steps and out into the sunshine. The girls talked excitedly between them, mostly about their brother's friends who might accompany him home, and their younger brother skipped rope ahead of them, all the way down the path to the rose garden.

Alice settled on a stone bench beneath a spray of white roses, somewhat disappointed at the children's chosen destination.

Rupert had finished his examination of the rose gardens before Alice even arrived at the castle. She knew from his sketches that he spent most of his time further away from the castle proper at this point in his studies.

It had been an age since she had caught more than a glimpse of him, and even that had been from the schoolroom window.

Perhaps she had misjudged their friendship. Or he had decided she was beneath his notice. Or...or something.

Her eyes stung a moment, but Alice brushed aside her feelings as foolishness. Then she opened her sketchbook and began work on her drawing of Lady Rosalind. She intended to gift the sketch to the girl for her upcoming birthday. Childhood was fleeting, and perhaps having it preserved in a sketch would gratify the girl when she grew up.

Alice removed her spectacles and rubbed at her eyes, then watched Rosalind with the eyewear still in her hand. Both of the duke's younger daughters were pretty, and would soon grow into beautiful women, likely to turn the head of every man from London to the farthest reaches of Europe.

For the present, Alice was happy to grant them the peace of their mother's gardens.

EVERY DAY THAT HE DID NOT SEE ALICE, RUPERT COUNTED AS dull. Despite the progress of his work, and his lively conversations on science with the duke, he missed the governess. He missed her observations on flowers and insects and people; he missed her quick smile and her wit.

Rupert rolled over in the grass of the meadow, a dandelion between his teeth as he stared upward at the summer sky.

He missed talking to her and listening when she talked.

In fact, it had impacted his work. When he ought to have studied the workings of a hornet's nest he found in the woods, he instead sketched more flowers for her to add color and gathered many more specimens of plants than was strictly necessary, just to send them to her.

Why could not a dinner guest fall ill again, making room at the table for Alice?

Perhaps that was an unkind wish, but it was in his mind. He had debated sending her a note, asking for a meeting, several times. As the silence stretched between them, he wondered if it would be wise. If they did not meet again naturally, and soon, he might go mad.

As a bachelor, he could hardly send personal notes to Alice when anyone might read them. Rupert wouldn't make her fodder for gossip. His work had kept him at the far reaches of the estate, and her duties as governess kept her with the children.

"It's possible I imagined it all," he said aloud to a bee that came to inspect his dandelion. The bee landed on Rupert's nose. "I know most consider me odd the moment I open my mouth."

The bee apparently thought the same, as it took flight and left him.

Talking to bees was a new low point in his life.

Rupert sat up, then drew his watch from his pocket to check the time. Three o'clock in the afternoon, with hardly any work to show for it.

Of course, he drew near the end of the project. At least, near to the end of making observations. He had only the woods left to explore, then he would compile his findings into a book for the duke and make a more abbreviated version of the work to submit to the Royal Society.

The most interesting part of his studies was nearly at a close. He would not even need to be present on the duke's property anymore. He could journey the sixteen miles back to his father's estate and finish writing up his discoveries there.

Perhaps never seeing Alice again.

He wanted to talk to Alice. He cared too much about her to leave without a word, without telling her that he—

He cared about her more than he had words to say.

Rupert rose and dusted himself off, then gathered up the basket full of little cages and his sketchbook. He slung his long butterfly net over his shoulder, then he turned and went slowly up the hill toward the formal castle gardens and the castle itself.

The structure was imposing, he reflected. If one did not know it had been built a decade before, one might suppose it to be a true work of Gothic architecture. Her Grace had done a fine job on the design. Thankfully, the interior was more modern and comfortable than buildings of greater age.

He missed his own home, though.

He trudged up through the wild gardens, the statue garden where he avoided looking in the direction of Aphrodite, then into the rose gardens.

He stepped through the hedges, around a large fountain, and into another section of roses surrounding a large elm tree.

Alice. His heart surprised him, singing her name in his thoughts the exact moment he saw her.

There she sat, on one of the stone benches, in perfect profile from where he stood. She was bent over her sketchbook, her bonnet casting shade upon her face, and her bare hand flying over the paper as she drew.

Rupert nearly dropped everything he held but came to his senses and put his belongings down carefully, instead. Then he tucked his hands behind his back and approached, moving slowly even though his heart raced at the very sight of her.

She came aware of him when he was still several feet away, her posture stiffening a moment before she turned her head to see him. For a long, horrid moment she appeared only surprised.

He had made a mistake. Overstepped. Perhaps been too forward—

Then she rose, dropping her sketchbook at once, and she crossed the distance between them until she was near enough to touch.

"Rupert," she said, her eyes glowing a clear, more stunning blue than he remembered. That was when he realized she did not wear her spectacles. Without the glass and metal to frame her blue eyes, they were magnificently beautiful, like the very sky he had stared at only moments before.

He bowed, not taking his gaze from hers. "Alice."

Then, despite the forwardness of such a remark, she said what he had thought the whole of the morning. "I have missed you terribly. Where have you been?"

A startled laugh escaped him, then he reached for her hand, reveling in the touch of her bare skin against his. "Here and there, my dear. You have received my flowers and sketches. You know exactly where I have been."

Her cheeks pinked and she nodded once. "In the meadow and the woods, then. I am afraid my duties have kept me inside, and with the children."

"While mine have kept me out-of-doors." He had eyes only for her, as the world around them momentarily ceased to exist. "I missed you, too," he admitted. "Though I did not know what to do about it."

"The day after tomorrow is my half day," she said, then her color deepened. "Oh, that was entirely too eager. Of course, you will be busy—"

"Busy spending time with you," he interjected quickly, feeling heat creep up his neck and into his ears.

Her shy smile made him adore her still more than he had before. Rupert drew a little closer and bent toward her.

"Mr. Gardiner," a young feminine voice shouted.

Alice stepped away, her eyes widening rather comically as she turned toward the children.

The three youngest members of the duke's brood stared at them, Lord James with a puzzled frown and the two girls with wide eyes and delighted smiles.

A colorful litany of obscure words paraded through Rupert's mind, but he forced himself to appear undisturbed as he gently released Alice's hand.

"My lord and ladies, I did not see you there."

"Apparently not," Lady Rosalind said, her grin widening.

Lady Isabelle elbowed her younger sister in the ribs. Then she curtsied prettily, prompting her siblings to greet him with better manners.

"We are so pleased to see you, Mr. Gardiner," Lady Isabelle said, all diplomatic politeness. "Unfortunately, we cannot stay to talk. Rosalind and I must attend to our mother, and we had better take James along with us. I am certain he has an appointment with our father before dinner."

The boy scowled up at his sister but did not contradict her. Rupert suspected Rosalind had given him a pinch at the elbow to ensure he went along with their contrived reason for leaving.

Alice frowned at her young charges. "I was not aware—"

"Never mind, Miss Sharpe," Lady Isabelle said quickly. "We will make our way back inside. Your enjoyment of the garden needn't end because we are called away." She curtsied again, then fairly dragged Lady Rosalind behind her, who in turn spurred Lord James into moving with a glare.

Alice's blush deepened, but she did not follow the children out of the garden with more than her gaze, her eyebrows pulling together in a frown. "Oh dear. That was not subtle at all."

"You really ought to teach them better acting skills," Rupert said, unable to help but tease her. "Surely that falls under the duties of a governess."

Alice faced him again, still appearing rather bewildered. "Rupert, what if they tell someone? If Her Grace thinks I am conducting private liaisons with gentlemen..." She let her words die away, concern darkening her eyes.

Rupert glanced the way the children had gone, then drew her with him into the shadows beneath the tree. "Somehow, I do not think they mean to spread gossip. It is easy enough to see those children adore you." His heart beat rapidly within his breast. "May I spend your half day with you?" Rupert took her other hand, holding both of them low and between them. "I would like to show you what I have studied, and I want to hear of how you have passed your days."

"I can hardly believe it," she said, tilting her head to the side as she teased him. "I thought insects held more interest for you than people."

"That is generally true." He released a rather dramatic sigh. "They are less complex, to be sure. But I find they do not carry on conversations very well. Only this afternoon, a bumblebee snubbed me when I tried to confide in him."

Alice's lips twitched upward. "Oh, dear. How rude of him."

"Terribly rude." Rupert bent a little closer, enthralled by the clear blue of her eyes. "Where are your spectacles?"

She tipped her chin upward. "On the bench."

"Do you not need them?" He asked, curious as he took in the pale tips of her eyelashes, which he had not noticed before that moment. They were as golden as her hair.

"Not all the time. It has become a habit to wear them." Her voice lowered, as though she shared a secret. "One of my relatives insisted I keep them on, because they made me appear plainer."

"Horrid person, whoever it was." Rupert released one of her hands in order to lay his palm against her cheek, causing her to shiver. "They do not make you plain at all. Nothing so simple could hide your beauty, my Alice."

Her breath shuddered. "Without them, you do look rather blurry when you stand so near."

That made him smile, but it did not prevent him from tipping his head lower. "That is a shame."

"Rupert?"

"Hm?"

"You are standing very close."

"Do you object?"

"No." She shivered. "I only wish you would *do* something about it."

He chuckled, then closed the remaining space between them to press his lips to hers in a gentle kiss.

She tasted sweeter than honey, and her lips were soft as rose petals. His arms went around her waist, and her hands fell upon his shoulders. Alice returned his kiss, gentle and uncertain at first, but as he deepened the kiss, her hands went around his neck.

When they broke apart, Alice's eyes remained closed an instant longer than his. "Rupert."

He kissed her forehead, and her eyes opened to stare up at him. "I am terribly sorry. I meant to wait. To make certain this was what you wanted." His fingertips brushed against her cheek. "We barely know one another, but I have felt this pull toward you almost since the moment we met."

"Even though I was so cross with you when you asked me to serve as your colorist?" she asked, her nose wrinkling at him. She did not pull away. Having her length pressed against him would soon drive him to distraction.

"Even then. I only wished to know you more. That is the real reason I asked for your help. I hoped it would mean more time in your company, more time to puzzle out what made you so indecipherable."

She laughed and stepped away. "And then I went to great lengths to stay away from you. I am sorry, Rupert. But—you cannot blame me. Surely. I am a governess." Her smile fell away. "I cannot afford dalliances of any kind. You must know that."

He shook his head. "That is not what this is."

She slipped further away from him, his hands falling from her waist. "I should go."

Rupert's heart ached. "Alice, you do believe me. I have no wish to play with your feelings, or to take kisses from you without consequence. There is more here between us. Being without you this long has made me understand—I care for you. Deeply."

"Then you will understand that I must be careful. One wrong step could leave me without a position in this house. Without a place to go. My reputation—"

"I understand," he hastened to say. "I can be discreet, Alice. But I cannot ignore this."

Her smile returned at last, though it was smaller. "Thank you. I will see you on my half day."

He wanted to snatch her back, to hold her again, but instead he nodded. "The day after tomorrow. The same time as before. Here."

Alice nodded. "Here. Good day, Rupert." She hurried away, stopping only to scoop up her sketchbook and gloves, her spectacles too. Then she disappeared from the garden, giving him one last glance over her shoulder as she went.

Rupert fell against the tree, his heart pounding in his chest.

He needed to visit home and speak to his parents. Soon. And Alice... He needed to determine how much she meant to him, and how much he meant to her. There was nothing more important in the world at that moment than studying what had grown between them, as unexpected as a rose in the middle of a marsh.

CHAPTER 16

Though Alice had not known Emma Arlen long, the companion had begun to feel like a friend. So the next day, while the children were busy with their art master and riding lessons, Alice went in search of the only woman in the castle who might offer her advice.

As a companion to the duke's daughter, Emma was in a similar position to Alice. She was a paid employee, but not exactly a servant, privy to much that happened within the family though not precisely a part of it.

Emma might understand Alice's muddled thoughts and equally confused heart.

Alice found Emma in a sitting room frequented by Lady Josephine. She was alone, as Lady Josephine was also working with the art instructor that afternoon.

When Alice came further into the room, Emma looked up from the book in her hands and immediately smiled in welcome.

"I do hope I am not interrupting," Alice whispered, looking around the room again to ensure herself they were alone. "But when you did not arrive with Lady Josephine for the painting session—"

"Oh, I try to avoid painting when possible. I am afraid it is not one of my talents." Emma brushed aside her shortcoming and rose from her chair, then gestured to a couch where both of them might sit comfortably. "Do join me. I thought about seeking you out, but you are always so busy planning the children's lessons that I had no wish to disturb you."

Alice settled next to her friend and spoke with sincerity. "I am always happy to make time for you." Then she rubbed at her forehead. "Though today I must beg your time and advice."

"This sounds almost serious." Emma leaned back against the curve of the couch's arm. "Is something amiss?"

Twisting her father's ring upon her thumb, Alice considered how to begin the conversation. "Will you keep what I tell you between us, Emma? I am—that is, I do not wish anyone else to know what I wish to tell you."

Emma gave one firm nod. "So long as what you have to say poses no harm to others, I will keep your secrets."

It was as reasonable an answer as one could hope for. Alice took in a deep breath before speaking.

"You have teased me about Mr. Gardiner before, if you will recall?"

Emma's lips twitched. "Indeed. I think he is rather enamored with you. I have never heard him speak with such warmth of a woman, of anyone, really. He admires your talent, and your person."

Alice clenched her hands together in her lap, feeling her cheeks grow warm. "He kissed me yesterday."

The other woman's mouth fell open. "What? When?"

The whole story came spilling out of Alice, rather like water from a fountain, and she wrung her hands as she told it. Then her concerns came next. "What if this means nothing to him? As kind and sincere as he is, he is a gentleman of means and importance. He is *friends* with the duke. I am only a governess. I have no connections of consequence. He cannot be serious about his affections." Her eyes filled with tears and she searched her sleeve for her handkerchief.

"Here, take mine." Emma thrust a clean handkerchief trimmed with lace into Alice's hand. "You poor dear. I understand you perfectly." Emma moved closer and put her arm about Alice's shoulders. "The world is a frightening place for a woman alone, and those in our position, reliant upon our reputation but without protectors, are even more vulnerable."

Alice nodded as she dabbed at her eyes. "I am thoroughly confused, too. I certainly like him. I have from the first time I met him, when I thought him a gardener." She laughed at the memory, though the sound was somewhat bleak. "And yesterday, when he said how much he missed me, and he kissed me—I wanted to believe him. But how can I? Emma, I am a poor nobody."

"And you are concerned he is toying with your feelings?"

Though she hesitated a moment, well remembering the sincerity of Rupert's eyes and tone, Alice answered with a weak shrug. "I think he has an affection for me. But he cannot understand how complicated it would be for either of us. What would people say about him marrying a governess?"

"Alice, that might be your current position, but you are also the daughter of a gentleman. Orphaned or not. And you *do* have family scattered all over England."

"I am not related to anyone of importance," Alice protested. "My dowry is a pittance, held by one of my uncles, but no one ever really expected me to marry."

"From what you have said before, they worried that you *would* marry, by stealing their own daughters' suitors." Emma sniffed disdainfully, then folded her arms tightly across her chest. "Horrid relatives, all of them. If they were so concerned about it, they should have given you a proper coming-out and married you off first."

The absurdity of that idea made Alice laugh through her tears, and soon Emma laughed too.

"Why are you a companion?" Alice asked when their mirth subsided. "I have never heard your story."

"It is not interesting." Emma glanced away, toward the windows. "My parents were friends with the duke and duchess, though untitled. I was an only child. My mother was expecting another child when they died. There was an accident. Their carriage overturned on a bridge."

"I am sorry." Alice's heart squeezed in sympathy. "Were you very young?"

"I was ten years old." Emma rubbed at her arms. "Lady Josephine and I are of a similar age. The duke and duchess took me in as a ward. I have an inheritance waiting for me. The funds will be released either when I wed or reach five and twenty, unmarried. The rest of what belonged to my father went to a cousin."

The ducal family had taken Emma Arlen in out of the kindness of their hearts, and then they had given her a purpose. Alice twisted the handkerchief in her hands. "What would you do in my position?"

For a long moment, Emma stared out the window before returning her gaze to Alice. "You want to fall in love with Mr. Gardiner, don't you?"

"But I cannot think we are suited—"

"Stop that." Emma slid closer and took both of Alice's hands. "You are suited. I have never seen a woman learn of his fascination with insects and then carry on a conversation about them with him." A sliver of humor entered her tone. "The only thing that worries you, it seems, is the acceptance of others. Of what others may think. Mr. Gardiner is a grown man. Let him worry over that. Be honest. Tell him how you feel and what concerns you."

Alice bit her lip and looked down at her father's ring. "His family could object."

"What is the worst thing that could happen, Alice?"

"The duke and duchess would find out, and think me a

woman of poor morals, and send me packing." Spoken so baldly, her fear rose more darkly before her. "Then what? What if my own family will not take me back? What if—"

Emma interrupted, sounding exasperated. "What if all our noses turn blue and fall off?"

Alice hiccoughed. "What?"

"You can sit here and wonder 'what if' all day, Alice Sharpe. But you will never know for certain until it happens. Until you try." Emma squeezed her hands again. "Be brave, Alice."

Alice lowered her chin. "I have spent all my life unwanted by my own family. How could Rupert want me?"

"*Rupert* sees the value in tiny creatures living in the garden. If anyone would recognize what a treasure you are, it would be someone like him." Emma embraced Alice. "My dear friend, your family is foolish. Trust me when I tell you that. And do stop your crying. Come, show me what you will wear tomorrow to meet Mr. Gardiner. Or *Rupert*, I should say."

Though her fears were still present, Alice quelled them as best she could. Together, they went to her room, and Alice withdrew the blue dress, made especially for her, and the loveliest thing she owned. If she had to be brave, she would dress well for the occasion.

CHAPTER 17

R upert paced beneath the elm tree the next day, rehearsing in his thoughts all that had passed between him and Alice two days previous.

Kissing her had proven marvelous. But she had rushed away with such haste, he had to wonder if he had done something wrong. Had he acted too hastily? He had never been very good with people—at least, not beyond the small, polite talk his parents had spent years teaching him to perform.

But Alice was different, wasn't she?

Rupert dropped his forehead against the rough bark of the tree trunk. After they went so long without seeing one another, he had reacted to her presence like a starving man placed at a well-laid table. His enthusiasm may well have overwhelmed her.

Then there was her concern about her position. Governesses likely could not court. He had never heard of a governess who had. Had he?

Some married, he thought. One of his own governesses had, but years after she had left his family. When he had grown past such an age to need a governess, she had sent a letter informing them of her news. At least, he thought he recollected that happening.

He started pacing again, until a snatch of bright blue caught his eye. Rupert stopped and stared as Alice entered the rose garden, her steps hesitant and an uncertain smile upon her face.

The blue gown was *not* something any of his governesses had *ever* worn. Dressed as she was, she put him in mind of butterflies, wildflowers, and summer skies all at once.

He came from beneath the tree, wearing his admiration openly. And in the instant his hand touched hers, Rupert quite forgot his worries. She had come. They would muddle through somehow.

"Will you walk with me?" he asked, gesturing out into the garden. "I wish to know everything about you."

"Everything?" She looped her arm through his, and her cheeks turned pink. "There is not all that much to tell, I'm afraid."

"How can that be, when you have lived more than twenty years in this world without me knowing of it?" Rupert might have sounded like a fool, but he hardly cared. He wanted to know her.

She began somewhat hesitantly. "My parents died when I was five years old, and I was raised by my relatives. By whomever could spare the room or had the ability to manage an additional child."

Rupert nodded as she spoke. "Like our friend, Geoffrey. I cannot think one child could cause all that much difficulty."

"One would think." She punctuated her sentence with a sad smile. "But parents will always put their own children first." Though she began reluctantly, her story wove around them as they walked. He asked the occasional question, but it soon became clear to him why she was reluctant to speak of her past.

Somehow, despite her kindness and cleverness, Alice had never been *wanted* by her family. Though she shared moments of happiness in her childhood, Rupert's heart ached for the little girl without a permanent home. She had never known when she might be shuffled from one household to another, or what the next family would be like. Would they treat her as family or a servant? Would they keep her for a year or only a month?

They walked down through the gardens, away from the structure of the rose hedges and the careful arrangement of statues. Through the sunken fountain's garden, where several frogs chirped and burbled happily to each other. Finally, they arrived at the meadow. Far enough away from the castle's windows that— Rupert hoped—Alice would be more at ease.

Rupert asked fewer questions, and they gradually fell into silence sitting upon the meadow grass.

Alice had removed her gloves to pluck at daisies, and her restless fingers wove them together. Rupert leaned back on his hands, watching in silence, her history heavy on his heart. He saw the ring she wore on her thumb flash once in the sunlight, silver and scarred with slight scratches from years of wear.

"The ring you wear," he murmured. "Where did it come from?"

She paused a moment, then put her daisy chain in her lap in order to slip the ring from her thumb. She held it out to him. "It was my father's. He used to give it to me when he went away. I barely remember him, but I remember he would put this ring on a chain, and I would wear it until he came home."

Rupert accepted it in his palm, noting the inside of the ring was smooth and bright from her wearing it. "Incredible that a child would not lose it," he said, trying for a lighter tone.

Then he slipped it momentarily on his finger, the metal still warm from her skin. Her hands were so slight, the ring fit the second smallest finger on his right hand. He took it off again and held it out to her. "A precious gift."

Alice stared at the ring, then looked up at him with a crease in her brow before she accepted it again. "It is only a silver ring. And look how much it needs polishing. I don't think I ever noticed until now how very damaged it is."

"A little polish from a jeweler would bring it to rights again." Rupert rolled onto his back and folded his hands across his middle. "You have lived such a life of hardship, Alice. I did not know—and now I understand. Will you forgive me for my ignorance? I can see now why you protect your position as fiercely as you do, and I would rather give up my project entirely than make you fearful of losing your place."

He turned his head to watch her profile as he spoke, his soul aching that he had caused her fear while in pursuit of his own plans. Yes, he dreamed of publishing a paper in the Royal Society, of joining their esteemed ranks. But to do so at the cost of her peace? It would be reprehensible.

It was too soon for him to tell her—admit to her—that he had started to imagine offering her a *different* place. One by his side. As his wife.

The word frightened and elated him, but he kept the thought to himself.

What would that do to the duke's regard for Rupert? Would he earn His Grace's ire in stealing away a governess all his children dearly loved?

THE SINCERITY WITH WHICH RUPERT SPOKE LIFTED A weight from Alice's chest. She lifted her daisy chain again, tucking another stem into the plait. Then she turned her gaze to him, where he rested in the grass, his stare upon her almost fierce as he waited for her to speak.

"I feel I know the family a little better now. The children and I get along well. I am not afraid of losing what I have here. At least, not regarding the work we do together." She plucked one more flower, adding a last bit of length to her chain before looping it back upon itself to make a crown.

Rupert watched her, his smile returning, softer now. "But you are concerned about what will happen if we are seen too often together. If I attempt to court you, as you deserve to be courted."

Alice's cheeks warmed and she nodded, letting the daisy crown fall to her lap. "When they took me on, the dowager duchess and her grace were both clear about my duties, and what I could not do. 'Fraternizing with men' was most certainly upon the list of actionable offenses." She tried to smile, but it felt weak to her. "Oh, Rupert. What am I to do?"

He sat up and took her hand from her lap, holding it between both of his. "Leave it to me, my dear. I will put some thought to the matter. Until then, I will make a heroic effort in refraining from showing my affection for you. In public, at least."

She peered up at him, seeing his crooked smile paired with the sincerity in his gaze. "Your affection for me?"

"You do not think I go about kissing every governess I meet, do you?" he teased. "I assure you, that distinction belongs to you alone. Forgive me for going about a courtship like a bumbling fool. But I have never—and this is the truth, dear Alice—I have never felt the slightest interest in another woman. Not like this."

"You only like me because I am not afraid of frogs or spiders," she countered, though a genuine warmth grew in her heart. "And I can color your flowers in better than you can."

Rupert laughed outright, the sound deep and joyful. Then he rolled onto his elbow to look up at her, his eyes dancing with humor and something else. Something that made Alice's stomach feel as though any number of beautiful white-winged moths had taken flight inside her.

"All of this is true, but those are not the *only* reasons." Rupert narrowed his eyes at her. "I like you, dear Alice, because you speak honestly, always. I like you because you care about little boys who fall from trees. I like you because you rescue frogs. I like you because there is intelligence in your eyes and in your words. I like you because being near you makes me happy, and I find myself wishing to prove, for you and perhaps because of you, that

I am a better man today than I was yesterday. Your company is the best I have ever enjoyed. I like you, Alice, because you are you."

What did a woman say to such things? These were not the compliments she had overheard her cousins' suitors bestow on their beauty. They were not frivolous remarks upon her appearance, or things that might be said of anyone.

"Have I rendered you speechless?" he asked, teasing her gently. "But you always have something witty to say to me."

Alice pressed her lips together and narrowed her eyes at him. Then she picked up her daisy crown and dropped it upon his head. "You are quite right to like me so much." Then she bent and kissed his cheek, though he moved as though he wished to catch her before she could withdraw. Alice laughed, pulling away quickly. "Thank you, Rupert. I do not think anyone has ever said so many kind things to me at once."

"It is customary, I think, for a lady to tell the gentleman who says such nice things that she likes him, too." He didn't touch the daisy crown, though it fell a bit over his forehead. He looked up at her rather like a child begging for sweets. "Or shall I work harder to earn your esteem, my lady?"

"I think you know I like you very well. As you do not go about kissing governesses, you ought to realize that I do not go about kissing gentlemen." Indeed. His kiss was the first she had ever received.

Rupert sat up, brushing off his sleeves. "I had better return you to your schoolroom, dear governess. As much as I wish to keep you to myself, the hour grows late."

Alice waited for him to stand, then he offered his hand to her. She stood and leaned into his shoulder for a moment, reveling in the feeling of being *wanted*. Her gaze fell upon the nearby woods and she shuddered.

"Is something wrong? You cannot be cold." Rupert put his arm around her shoulders, holding her close.

"The woods. I have never liked them. When I was a little girl, no more than six or seven, I played with cousins in the woods near an uncle's home. They all knew the paths and trees, and they left me there. No one thought to look for me for hours and hours." Alice still had dreams about being lost in the trees, with night coming on, all alone.

"I wish I could speak my mind to all your horrid relatives," Rupert murmured against her hair. "I would never forget you, Alice. You are too precious, too wonderful, to be away from my thoughts for even an instant."

Alice laid her cheek against his chest and closed her eyes, drinking in his words, and hoping very much that they would always prove true.

CHAPTER 18

The summons from Rupert's father came only three days after the walk with Alice. Rupert had tried to snatch glimpses of her often, as she had promised to take the children on more walks in the afternoons, he could at least pass by and offer her a smile and wave.

But when he received the letter from Mr. Reginald Gardiner, requiring Rupert come home at once, he could not find Alice anywhere.

Billings packed most of Rupert's things, and set about loosing the insects in Rupert's cages from the bedroom window.

"What could Father mean, sending me this?" Rupert asked, not for the first time. He read over the letter again, having just come in from checking the schoolroom for Alice. It had been empty of her and the children both.

Billings made no reply, merely continued to release a damselfly who seemed reluctant to leave her cage.

Rupert read the note aloud, determined to gain a response from *someone*. Even if it was only his valet.

"*Son, I require your presence at home, at once. Make your excuses to His Grace. I will require you to take your leave of his fine home for a week, at least. He will understand. There are matters here that require your attention, and it will be to your benefit to attend your mother and I."*

He dropped the letter inside his open trunk, which Billings filled with clothing. "What can he mean, trying to be mysterious? Why not come out and say what could be so important that he must take me from the castle?"

"I could not say, sir," Billings said at last, sounding irritated that Rupert required him to give an answer at all. "But he has never sent for you in such a manner before. It must be important."

Could his father's reasons be as important as Alice if he left without taking his leave of her? She had never known when she would leave a household, or when someone she cared about would leave her behind. Rupert could not, and would not, do that to her.

"I need to write a letter." He went to his desk, then turned abruptly to Billings. "Stop packing a moment. Go and see if you can find out where Miss Sharpe and the children have gone. I cannot find her, nor anyone who knows where she must be. But someone in this blasted castle will know."

Billings started at the frustration in Rupert's tone, but Rupert did not care. He had other things to worry about. Things like Alice's trust, her heart, her affection.

But what could he say in a letter that would explain his abrupt departure? How could he make her understand something he did not understand himself?

My Dear Alice—

He tore that off the top of the paper. If anyone else found the letter, he had no wish to put Alice in a difficult position. He groaned. Why could she not be in the schoolroom where she was supposed to be?

Miss Sharpe,

I am afraid the continuation of our project must wait for a time. My father has called me home without delay. I regret that I cannot take leave of you in person, but I hope to return soon.

He stared at the inadequate words, hating them. But what more could he say that would not be misconstrued by prying eyes?

We will finish the catalog together. As I promised.

That was the best he could do. Rupert folded the note and stuck it in the flowers he had gathered earlier that morning. A stack of his sketches were beside the blooms and stems, waiting for her to apply her paint.

Now to take leave of the duke, claiming filial duty as his only excuse for leaving everything near finished, but not near enough.

ALICE FOLLOWED ALONG BEHIND THE DUKE'S THREE youngest children, listening as Lady Josephine and her companion carried on a conversation at her side.

"I cannot abide most of Simon's friends. They are all abominably full of themselves," Lady Josephine complained from beneath her parasol.

"You would not say the same of your brother, and I cannot believe he surrounds himself with men so different from himself." Emma paused before an attractive display at the grocer—summer fruits were artfully arranged to spill out a tipped basket.

The children had stopped just ahead to speak to a boy about the same age as Lady Isabelle. Even Lord James looked happy to see the youth.

"We ought to bring your mother some cherries," Emma remarked. "These are the first I have seen this season."

"Oh, that is a fine idea. Go inside and purchase whatever they have." Josephine waved her friend and companion inside the shop, then she turned her attention to Alice. "You must think me dreadful, complaining about Simon's friends this way. My brother is a man of good character, but sometimes I feel as though the men surrounding him are only his friends because of his title."

"An understandable suspicion," Alice admitted, keeping watch over the children from the corner of her eye. "A future duke holds nearly as much power as a prince. I am certain he is a discerning gentleman, and your concern for him does you credit, my lady."

Lady Josephine rested her parasol upon one shoulder. "I feel that I am forever questioning the motives of others. I suppose I have a suspicious nature. For instance, I should dearly like to know what has become of your friendship with Mr. Gardiner." She narrowed her eyes, an impish gleam to them.

With her cheeks warming, Alice struggled to sound unmoved by the mention of Rupert's name. "I suppose you could say it is going well. His project continues to be of interest."

"His project." Lady Josephine twirled the handle of her umbrella. "I rather wonder if he has not made wooing *you* his project, Alice."

"My lady," Alice protested, feigning a gasp.

"He speaks of you often, though I can tell he does not realize it." Lady Josephine shaded her eyes to peer into the grocer's shop, likely checking on Emma's progress with the cherries. "Only last evening at dinner he said how fortunate my brother and sisters are to have you seeing to their education."

"He only meant to be kind." Alice tugged her wrist-length gloves more snugly beneath the long sleeves of her chocolate colored gown.

Emma returned, the basket on her arm now bearing a smaller container of cherries. "I asked for two pounds of cherries to go to the kitchens, but I brought these to give to your mother now."

The children were fetched, and they all began the walk back to the castle. Lord James hurried ahead of all of them, intent on taking a purchase of candy up to his room to squirrel it away.

The ladies kept up a conversation on neighbors and cherries, and Alice felt, for the first time in ages, as though she belonged. Yes, her position as governess put her beneath both ladies in her company, but they did not treat her as a lesser person. The children were happy. Her life had purpose.

And, most of all, Rupert had feelings for her. He wished to court her. She smiled to herself, joy in her heart as the castle came into view upon the hill.

Almost, Alice could imagine herself a princess arriving at the grand home, stepping out as a guest rather than an employee.

"We must take the cherries to Mama," Lady Josephine said when they entered the smaller foyer, a butler and maid taking their things. "Then we shall come have tea with you, Alice."

Alice followed behind Lady Isabelle and Lady Rosalind. They entered the children's wing at the same moment Lord James dashed through his door. The girls disappeared into their room to lay aside their own purchases.

When Alice entered the schoolroom, she immediately noted the vases of flowers in the middle of the large circular table. A leather folder, thick with drawings, waited for her, too.

She put her hand on the leather flap and pulled it over, holding her breath in anticipation of a letter or note accompanying the sketches. Though they were hardly love letters, she treasured each word Rupert wrote to her.

But there was nothing written accompanying the sketches.

Alice blinked and moved the pictures, fanning them out, but still saw no note. Hm. Perhaps Rupert wished to give her instruction in person.

Then she examined the flowers, smiling to herself all the while. There were several wild flowers she would need to color in first. They would droop and lose their colors before the more cultivated blooms from the gardens.

Lady Josephine and Emma arrived at nearly the same moment as the maid bearing the tea tray. Alice opened the door wide and stood aside to allow everyone inside.

"Oh, Alice." Emma stopped beside Alice, eyebrows high upon

her forehead. "Do you know why Mr. Gardiner left in such a hurry?"

For the space of a heartbeat, Alice's world froze. "What do you mean?"

"Mama told us he took his leave of the duke not a quarter hour ago," Lady Josephine said from where she had already seated herself at the table. "Oh, dear. We assumed you would know the details, so I did not ask Mama for more information."

"No." Alice's body went cold, her mind numb. "But—Mr. Gardiner left? The castle?"

Emma's expression changed to a deep frown. "He returned home. His father's estate is sixteen miles west of here."

"He took his valet, and his things, Mama said." Lady Josephine started pouring out for them, wearing a frown of her own. "I felt certain he would have told you he was leaving. Perhaps he sent a note?" She looked to the flower sketches.

"Not that I have seen." Alice walked slowly to the table, lowering herself into a chair, not truly aware of her actions. "The flowers and sketches came without a note. I had no idea he planned to go anywhere. He did not tell me anything."

After a moment of unsettling quiet, Lady Josephine passed Alice a cup of tea. "I shall ask Papa for you."

That idea startled Alice into thought at last. "No. Please, do not trouble the duke on my account." She forced a smile, though she felt how the edges of her mouth trembled. "I am certain there is no cause for concern. Mr. Gardiner must be needed at home."

But why had he not left her a note? Or some word of his departure? Could he not have waited to take his leave of her? A quarter of an hour meant he had left the house only minutes before she returned from the outing with the children.

Their conversation the day previous, his gentle words and open affection, had given Alice every reason to hope—to hope he meant what he said. But to leave the duke's home, and their project, with nary a word of instruction or reassurance of his return—

Stop being silly, Alice told herself sternly, hiding her fear behind the rim of her teacup.

Emma's expression changed from one of curiosity to something more like sympathy. She turned her gaze to the flowers on the table and reached for one, lightly touching an unfurled leaf. "What is this flower called, Alice? I cannot say that I know it."

Alice cleared away her thoughts, promising herself she would not dwell on a thing she could not know.

Why had Rupert left without so much as a word of farewell? Not even a written one?

CHAPTER 19

The excellent condition of the roads and lack of summer rain allowed Rupert's carriage, borrowed from the duke, to arrive well before dinner. Two hours of travel had not at all dampened his curiosity or dimmed his hope that Alice would understand.

Rupert exited the coach, Billings behind him giving directions to the footmen, and he took in his father's estate with a critical eye. It was not even a quarter of the size of the duke's castle. But it was more comfortable than the castle would ever be, with a more welcoming air, because it was home. He climbed the steps to enter between the two wide columns that marked the doorway, then stepped into the hall. The floor was finely polished wood instead of marble, the staircase not sweeping but elegant enough for his tastes.

His mother appeared at the top step. "Rupert, darling! Welcome home." She came down, one hand upon the rail, and he met her halfway with a quick embrace.

"Mother, I have missed you."

She leaned away and shook a finger at him. "You ought to have come home more, young man. The duke's house is not so far as to make a visit every fortnight impossible. Or you could have written."

"I know," he admitted, one arm around his mother's shoulders as he turned so they might both walk up the stairs. "I am afraid I have been rather caught up in my work."

He had been head and shoulders taller than her since his four-teenth birthday, and walking with her thus was quite natural. Not many English boys could boast of having a mother such as his—a woman of understanding and love who had never felt the need to smother her son with either.

"That is hardly an excuse. I never allowed your father to neglect me in his pursuits of science, and I shall not allow it of you." She parted from him at the top of the stairs. "Whatever will happen if you find a wife and she thinks you prefer your insects to her company?"

An image of Alice's amused smile overtook Rupert's thoughts, and he had to chuckle at his mother's question. "I will do my utmost to ensure my wife knows the place she holds in my heart."

Something about his tone appeared to startle his mother, as she folded her hands before her and drew herself up, peering into his eyes. "I think that is the first time you have met the subject of a wife with a smile."

Rupert cleared his throat and diverted his gaze. "Where is Father hiding today? The urgency of his summons made me believe he would be waiting for me at the gates."

"You know your father. Anything to do with the Royal Society..." She let her words trail away with a wave. "He is in his study."

Rupert's eyebrows lifted, and he turned toward the corridor leading to his father's sanctum. The Royal Society? His father had mentioned nothing to do with the body of science-minded gentlemen in his note.

"Oh, go on with you. Neither of you are fit company until you have discussed all things genus and species." She gave Rupert a gentle push on the shoulder. "Have it out, then we can talk of other things at dinner."

Rupert dropped a quick kiss upon his mother's cheek. "You are an angel, Mother." He swept off to his father's study, his mind turning over the possibilities of scientific news important enough to merit interrupting his stay at Castle Clairvoir. A new discovery, perhaps? Some proclamation made by their greatest patron, the Regent?

He knocked on the sturdy oak door, the same he had approached day after day in his childhood to proudly show his father some new thing found in the grove of trees near their home. Bird feathers his father always knew the origin of, acorn tops, and any number of insects.

Thankfully, though his father thought the most of birds, he never discouraged Rupert's curiosity of the world around him.

"Enter," came the command from the other side of the door.

Rupert stepped into the study, posture correct and grin wide. "Greetings, Father."

Reginald Gardiner rose from behind his desk and came around the corner of the impressive piece of furniture. "Rupert, my boy. You are here with such speed. Thank you for that." He extended his hand in welcome, and Rupert took it in a firm shake.

"You raised me a dutiful son, Father. When you asked that I come with all speed, I obeyed." Despite what it meant to take his leave of Alice in such a shoddy way. Rupert tried to ignore his guilt—he *had* left the note, after all. That would be enough. "Though your summons was distressingly vague. Are you in good health?"

"The best." Father stood back and thumped a fist against his chest, over his heart. Only twenty-three years separated father and son, as his parents had married young. Rupert had the privilege of inheriting his father's fine features and stature, the two of them close enough in appearance that people could not help connecting them. "I trust His Grace was not too reluctant to let you leave him?"

Rupert shrugged, remembering the perplexed frown of the duke. "His Grace understands familial duty."

"Of course, of course. Here, sit down. I need you to read something." He went to his desk and opened the top drawer while Rupert lowered himself into one of the comfortable chairs on the other side. "I just received this letter from the clerk of the Royal Society yesterday."

Rupert accepted the creased paper, giving it his full attention as he read.

To Mr. Reginald Gardiner, Fellow of the Royal Society,

Greetings,

I am staying in Leicester, near your home in South Croxton. As we have had occasion to exchange letters on your observations of bird behavior during certain astronomical events, I hope you will not think it presumptuous of me to ask if I might pay you a call.

It is always a pleasure to meet with other members of our esteemed society to discuss the world of science and our respective disciplines.

Sincerely,

Mr. Stephen Lee

Clerk & Librarian of the LRS

Rupert read through the letter again. "Mr. Lee is coming here? When?"

"Day-after-tomorrow. I have invited him to stay for two days." Father puffed out his chest with pleasure. "It is nearly as good as receiving a visit from Sir Joseph Banks." His father spoke the name of the president with reverence, as most in the scientific community would. Sir Joseph had been president for forty years and had inducted Reginald Gardiner into the Society as a fellow when Rupert was still a boy.

"But what does Mr. Lee's coming have to do with me?" Rupert returned the letter to his father. As the Society had yet to invite Rupert to join as a fellow and had rejected several articles he had attempted to publish through their journal, Mr. Lee's arrival obviously had nothing to do with him.

"As clever as you are, my boy, can you not work it out?" His father tossed the letter to the desk before leaning against it, folding his arms over his chest. "This is your chance. Mr. Lee has served as clerk and librarian of the Society for years. He is trusted by Sir Joseph and well known to every person on the membership committee. To have his acquaintance will bring you another step closer to joining the society yourself."

Rupert stared at his father, working out the logic for himself. "But—the Royal Society has spoken of limiting membership of late, due to the very fact that too many people are allowing friends and acquaintances in to give them distinction, despite their lack of scientific bend or knowledge. As much as I would like to be published, I cannot think they will allow me in when my work has been trivial compared to other men."

"Trivial?" His father snorted. "There is no such thing as any part of nature being *trivial*. This is the world in which we live, Rupert. Every blade of grass could be of importance, and we simply lack the understanding to see it at present. Insects and flowers in a field might hold the keys to unlocking mysteries of health, or illness, or cure famine and hunger. What have I been teaching you all this time if it is not that?"

Rupert scrubbed his hands through his hair, remembering Alice and their last afternoon together in the meadow. While he had never questioned the importance of gaining the Royal Society's approval before, at the moment, he could only think on leaving Alice. But she would understand, surely.

"How long do you need me here?"

"How long—? Rupert, you disappoint me." Father shook his head slowly, wincing as he did. "Meeting Mr. Lee is important. I expect you to stay as long as he does. Get to know him and share your studies with him. He is on the committee for approving items for publication. When you tell him that the Duke of Montfort is one of your patrons, it will undoubtedly help your case."

And see his work published in the journal, with Alice's accompanying artwork and credit.

Rupert owed it to all of them, himself, the duke, and especially Alice, to put his work forward at any possible opportunity.

The day after tomorrow, plus two more days, and then taking his leave after that, meant staying with his family for five days.

That wasn't too long.

If his father's hopes proved true, if making Mr. Lee's acquaintance furthered Rupert's ambitions as a naturalist, then it would not be time ill spent.

"I will happily assist you in hosting Mr. Lee." Rupert rose to stand, his father doing the same and matching him in height. "The duke will understand. I need to write him, of course, and inform him of my return."

His father clapped a hand on Rupert's back. "Wonderful. Now, let us find your mother. She will have questions about the duchess's new style of decoration. Your mother has been after me for weeks to recover the chairs in her sitting room."

Rupert allowed his father to lead the way, happy enough to be home that his smile was genuine. Even if his heart tugged at him and urged him to return to Alice as soon as possible.

CHAPTER 20

The day the duke's eldest son came home, Alice received word that the family would breakfast together. Her duty was to assist the nursery maid in seeing the children were well dressed and prepared to enjoy the meal with the duke, his heir, the duchess, and any guests trailing the heir. Simon Dinard, bearing the honorary title Earl of Farleigh, was apparently a favorite of the entire family.

"Simon always brings back presents," Lord James informed Alice, while she tried to make him hold still long enough to comb his hair. He wore a miniature version of a gentleman's attire, looking every inch the duke's son except for a cowlick above his left eyebrow. "Last time, it was the theater for the marionettes. And he sent me the clockwork horse for my birthday."

Alice tried to hide her amusement at his enthusiasm. "I hope you enjoy seeing your brother for his own sake, too."

"He's a jolly enough brother, for all he's ancient. I think he's older than you, Miss Sharpe." The boy screwed up his face. "How old *are* you, anyway?"

Lady Isabelle laughed from the doorway to his room. "James, you should never ask a lady her age!"

"Why not?" Lord James fixed Alice with a curious stare. "People ask me how old I am all the time."

Lady Rosalind had joined her sister at the door. "Because you are a little boy."

Thankfully, both sisters were properly turned out in their loveliest morning gowns. Their shared maid had seen to their hair, too, rendering them lovely young ladies. It occurred to Alice, quite suddenly, that the large party of friends their brother traveled with might well one day include those that would marry her charges. If his friends were in their early twenties, a match might be made for the fourteen-year-old Lady Isabelle in another four or five years.

The upper nobility tended to marry later than the middle and lower classes. Still. The possibility was there.

Alice cleared her throat and brought them all back to the point. "I am old enough to have you in my charge, Lord James. That is all you need know." She finally tamed the lock of hair, though she doubted it would remain in place once the boy began his usual antics. "All of you go down to breakfast and do mind your manners. Be clever and polite so your parents will know I am doing my best."

They replied with their usual "Yes, Miss Sharpe" together, then went down the corridor, laughing and talking of their excitement to see their brother again.

Alice leaned against the doorway, and she watched a moment as the nursery maid tidied up the young lord's bed. Her name was Jenny, but beyond the occasional "yes, miss" and "no, miss," she had little to say to Alice.

For a moment, Alice imagined what it might be like to count the young girl as a friend. To speak of the children in their joint care, perhaps laugh about Lord James's antics and Lady Rosalind's continual talk of courtship.

She moved away, down to the schoolroom, where she had her

vase of flowers and a sheaf of sketches to cover in paints and inks until the paper plants were all the correct hues.

An hour of careful work left her eyes strained, even behind the spectacles which aided her in such close work. She sat back and removed the wire-framed glasses to massage her temples. With nearly two hours until the children returned, Alice had time to spare. Almost as much as she would on a half-day.

Alice stowed away the paints and sketches, then she went in search of another occupation. Something to let her eyes rest. And, feeling rebellious, she left her spectacles off.

They were not strictly necessary, and perhaps the strain upon her eyes had as much to do with wearing the glasses when it was unnecessary as it did concentrating on detailed painting.

With that justification as her shield against censure, Alice left the children's corridor and went down the long picture gallery. The duke's ancestors, and a rendering of the scowling regent, watched her cross the grand carpet all the way to the main staircase.

Although permitted to use the sweeping marble steps, doing so without the children always felt a touch wicked. Governesses were not to be seen except as they were required to be in attendance of their pupils.

But no one saw her, servant or otherwise, and she slipped directly out the main door.

Alice wandered down the long, curving lane that brought travelers up to the castle. She had not spent much time on that side of the grounds. All of her time with the children, and with Rupert, had been on the opposite side, in the gardens.

The pretty lawns of green on either side of the drive were dotted with sheep, and a few dairy cows in the distance. The whole of the scene penetrated her lonely heart. The whole of the world stretched around her, and no one noticed or cared where she walked or where she went.

As it had been the entirety of her life.

Until Rupert.

He had noted her, remarked on her intelligence, then praised her talent and made use of it. Not to be cruel, or to further his ambitions, but in a sincere effort to work with someone he deemed *interesting*. Then he saw more.

He saw *her*.

Alice caught sight of a daisy growing along the drive, tall and slim among the grass. A little bee hovered near a moment before landing, causing the flower to sway. Would Rupert know what sort of bee it was? Would he think it worthy of a sketch, or had he already captured the likeness of one of the bee's sisters?

Alice's smile twitched, then she had to laugh. Rupert had seen her, had noticed her, because he was in the habit of paying attention to details and creatures others deemed inconsequential. Daisies and wildflowers, moths and spiders, Rupert saw them all. He saw beauty and fascination in things others walked by without notice.

She had to have faith that a man with such an ability, even if he had left without word, would not forget her in his time away.

Even if he had been away for over a week.

And she missed him.

"No one told me the family had any members of the fairer sex as guests," a deep voice said from behind.

Alice whirled around, a hand coming up to her throat. She had not heard the tall gentleman approach. He wore black riding boots and a dark blue coat, a tall black hat, and a broad grin.

She dropped her gaze to the ground at once, as she had been taught to do since girlhood when confronted with a man not her relative or servant. "Pardon me, sir. I am the governess."

He would scoff and dismiss her. They always did.

"The governess? How fortunate for His Grace's children. All my tutors were middle-aged men with scowls and foul breath. You are quite pretty."

He stepped closer. "I am Mr. Briant."

It was not like when she met Rupert. The weight of this man's gaze was far heavier and unwanted.

"Miss Sharpe." She ought to have worn her spectacles. Perhaps that would have put him off. "If you will excuse me, I should return to my post." She started to walk around him, keeping several feet of empty air between them.

"I will walk with you." He matched her steps, coming closer than necessary. "I came with Lord Farleigh from London. He promised sport in the country."

Ah, a friend of the heir. That explained his presence. But not the way he cast his gaze upon her.

Alice nodded tightly. "I hope you enjoy your time here, sir."

His words took on a sly tone. "Between the pretty maid who lit the hearth in my room this morning, and someone as unexpected as you, I am certain I will."

Her cheeks warmed. "I am the governess, sir."

"And I am certain someone as lovely as you could teach me a few things."

They had reached the archway which led to the carriage house. Alice had turned their steps in that direction, all too aware of how empty the entry to the castle had been moments before.

She needed people. Witnesses. Because as strict as her family had been with her, several of her female relations had impressed upon Alice her reticence to be near some men was as important to Alice's well-being as it was to her cousins' prospects.

But the covered path to the carriage house, a place which allowed guests to exit vehicles and be certain of keeping dry no matter the weather, appeared as abandoned as the foyer.

And Mr. Briant stepped closer to her. "Last time I stayed at a country house, a most beautiful companion to the eldest daughter made it her responsibility to see to my...entertainment." The quiet emphasis on the final word as he spoke it, the shadow that appeared in his eyes, did not prepare her for his next move.

Mr. Briant grabbed her wrist and pulled Alice to a stop, then forced her back a step into a pillar. Where they stood, only someone entering either end of the covered path would see her—would see whatever Mr. Briant meant to do.

Alice's voice shook. "Sir, I cannot allow this. Let me go at once. I am under the duke's protection—"

The darkness in the man's eyes deepened and his lips curled sideways in a knowing smile. "Has His Grace claimed you for himself? Is that why he hired such a pretty little thing to cluck over his children in the nursery?" He bent low and kept her wrist in his bruising grip. "He is a very good host, you know. I doubt he will mind sharing—"

Alice cut off his words with a sharp slap. Which startled him enough that the horrid man released her wrist.

With only moments to use, Alice twisted away and ran for the entrance they had passed through. It was closer, and there were windows facing that way. Someone might see, someone might come—

She stumbled into the daylight, and into a broad chest, at the same moment Mr. Briant's hand closed on the back of her gown.

Alice looked up, hoping a groom or footman had appeared—

But she looked into the face of the Duke of Montfort himself.

"Miss Sharpe," he said, tone crisp. "Mr. Briant."

The man's steps skidded backward, and Alice stumbled into a curtsy likely every bit as muddled as she felt. The duke had caught her fleeing a man. A man who had implied horrid things about her. A man, given the way he had acted, rather used to getting his way.

Alice's heart thudded with painful force against her ribs. "Your Grace."

"Good morning, Your Grace." Mr. Briant sounded not at all penitent or upset.

Alice raised her eyes to the duke again, her lips parted to speak, but what would she say? Could she tell him of the attack against her, of the man—the duke's own guest—implying such vial things about her person and his expectations? A woman's voice against a man's was difficult enough—but an employed woman's testimony against a gentleman's?

Her throat closed up, she closed her mouth, and she remained in her deep curtsy.

"Miss Sharpe, it is fortunate that I found you." The duke's tone remained neutral but ignoring the greeting of his guest had to mean something. Didn't it? "I wish to show my son the work you have completed for the catalog of the gardens. Did Mr. Gardiner leave behind any of the drawings?"

Alice sensed escape and spoke eagerly. "Yes, there are several in the schoolroom that I have finished coloring only this morning. I can fetch them—"

"No, no. You must join the family. The children are adamant that you meet Simon. We can send someone for the sketches." Then he held his hand out to her.

The duke. Offered her his hand.

Alice's head went dizzy with relief and fear all at once. The duke had never even spoken to her directly before. Yet here he called her by name, addressed her with respect before another man, and offered her escort to safety.

Rupert had said the duke and the duchess were kind. But she had not thought someone so far above her in status would ever deign to pay her notice.

She slipped her hand into his, and the duke turned to lead them back through the door. He did not invite Mr. Briant to follow, so the man could not impose his company on the duke. It was near enough a cut-direct that Alice trembled at the retribution Mr. Briant might enact upon her.

The duke stepped inside the door, and a footman—wherever had he been when she needed him there?—closed the door behind them.

"There now, Miss Sharpe." The duke turned to look down at her, a gentle expression upon his noble face. He looked exactly like his portrait hanging at the top of the stairs in the family wing —tall, broad-shouldered, with dark hair starting to gray at the temples. He had a long nose, but his cheekbones and strong chin balanced it well. "You are safe."

Alice went cold from her fingertips to her toes, but her cheeks grew hot. "Your Grace, I did not mean for anything to happen. I was surprised. I didn't expect—" And then the sob broke free of her, and Alice pulled her hand from his gentle grasp to cover her mouth with both palms.

The duke remained silent while she fought for control over her emotions, but his expression was nothing but kind. He spoke with softness when she grew quiet again. "I have three daughters, Miss Sharpe. All of whom care for you. I have raised my sons to conduct themselves honorably. James saw you were distressed. I came at once."

Her jaw fairly hit the ground between them. "Lord James?"

"He looked out the dining-room window." The duke pointed to the floor above. "And said that it appeared you were being chased. I agreed and came. You are, at my word, a member of my household and under my protection. Mr. Briant will be gone before noon." He sighed deeply and looked up the stairs. "And I must have a word with my eldest about the company he keeps."

Then the Duke of Montfort offered her his arm. "I am certain there are people waiting for us, Miss Sharpe. Will you join my family upstairs?"

Alice nodded once, hardly believing how a nightmare had transformed into a splendid dream. How else could she explain the quick reversal of her situation only moments before?

If—no, *when* Rupert returned, she would tell him how right he was to trust and esteem the duke.

CHAPTER 21

"Father, I have to go. I have already been away too long." Rupert checked his watch. If he left in the next hour, he would arrive at Castle Clairvoir in time to find Alice before dinner.

His father glanced over the edge of the book he read, seated in his favorite chair of the library. "But Mr. Lee is still here, and he is highly interested in your studies."

"I doubt that." Rupert released a frustrated sigh. "I think he is only being polite and enjoying the fine accommodations. Perhaps he's interested in *your* observations of the effect a full moon has on nesting birds."

Mr. Lee had a fine scientific mind, as the librarian and clerk of the Royal Society must, but his own interests were nearer the heavens than the creeping things of the earth. Rupert could not fault the man for his preference, but it certainly made his journey to his parents' home feel wasteful.

Mother sat in a chair nearby, perusing a women's journal. "Mr. Lee does enjoy talking about the moon. Perhaps you might find something to discuss with moths and moonlight, Rupert." Her tiny smile of amusement was her only indication of teasing.

How did he make them understand? Rupert needed to take his leave. Especially given how unsettled he had become that morning. Something was wrong. Something to do with Alice. He felt it in his heart.

He had jolted out of bed, later than usual due to entertaining neighbors the night before, with Alice's name on his lips.

Their attachment was too new, their affection for one another not even in its larva state—

He winced.

"I really must cease comparing *everything* to insects," he muttered to himself.

His father snapped the book closed. "What was that?"

Perhaps it would be better to borrow from his father's vernacular. "Fledgling state sounds far better than larva," he observed.

"I agree, but both are juvenile states for their respective creatures." Father tilted his chin down and fixed Rupert in place with a deep frown. "But what does that have to do with anything?"

Rupert took in a shaky breath. He noted his mother put down her journal and looked at him with as much curiosity as his father. He had to tell them.

"I have developed feelings for a young woman."

"Developed feelings?" His father dropped the book to the floor with a thump.

Mother laughed. "Oh, Rupert. You make it sound like a fever." She rose from her chair. "But this is wonderful. No wonder you are so eager to be on your way. Was she a houseguest of the duke's?"

"No." Rupert shifted his gaze from one parent to the other.

"A neighbor?" His father guessed next.

"No, not a neighbor."

His mother gasped and put a hand to her heart. "*Not* the duke's daughter! Never say that. Oh, I could not at all be the mother-in-law to a duke's daughter."

Rupert groaned and shoved a hand through his hair. "No,

Mother. Not Lady Josephine. You don't know her—but she is clever, and witty, and the loveliest woman I have ever met. Her name is Alice Sharpe." He had told Alice her status as a gentleman's daughter had not changed with her position as a governess. Would his parents see things as he hoped?

"Out with it, boy. Is she spoken for? Too proud to court you?" His father was on his feet now too, eyes bright. "Or has she accepted you and you've kept the whole of it a secret?"

Rupert spoke his answer slowly, and clearly. "She's the governess."

For the space of two heartbeats, his parents said nothing.

Then his mother emitted a sound he had never heard before—something between a shriek and a yelp—before she took hold of Rupert's arm. "Are you engaged to marry? When will we meet her? What about her family? Do they approve of the match?"

"Let the boy talk, Mariah." Father's chest puffed out rather like a male chickadee's—though Rupert kept the comparison to himself. "Tell us everything, Rupert. Before your mother flies apart."

Rupert put his hand over his chest. "I sincerely have nothing more to tell. I have *not* declared myself, or asked for her hand, because this is all very new. I had barely spoken to her—barely expressed my interest—when I received your note. And now I have been here for nearly a fortnight—"

"Keeping her a secret." His mother glowered at him. "Rupert, you know full well that it is our fondest hope for you to fall in love. How else am I to have grandchildren?"

Rupert's weak laugh was his only answer to that. His mother was not as vocal on the subject as some, but he *did* know how much she wanted a daughter-in-law, and grandchildren running about the house. His birth had been difficult for his mother, and damaging. She had never carried another babe to term after his birth, and eventually no longer fell pregnant.

Rather than grow apart, or grow bitter, his parents had

lavished all their love upon him. Perhaps it had made him a little odd, to grow up with his father for a playmate and his mother his most frequent companion. Rupert never doubted their love.

"Get out," his father said, pointing to the door. "Get back there at once and woo the lady properly. When a man finds the match to his heart, the woman's whose heart song is a match for his, he must not lose her."

"But—I barely—that is, it's difficult to court a governess." Finally given permission to leave, Rupert was torn between running out the door and laying all his troubles at his parents' feet. They would have answers he did not.

"There is always difficulty, son." His father wrapped an arm around Mother's shoulders. "It is up to you to work your way through it or around it."

Mother's enthusiasm had waned somewhat. "If your affection is so new, a fledgling thing barely ready for flight, you must treat it gently. You owe it to yourself and the young lady to see how far you might go." She narrowed her eyes. "How does she feel about your insects?"

The first time they met, she captured a butterfly from his shoulder. She spoke of spiders and butterflies and bees all with the same respect and curiosity. She rescued frogs from castles and loosed them into ponds.

"She understands them," Rupert said, a touch of awe in his tone. "And, I think, she understands me."

In short order, Rupert climbed into the family carriage with Billings and a trunk full of his things. His parents stood on the steps, along with a bewildered Mr. Lee, waving Rupert away to good fortune.

The worry that had settled in his chest lessened.

Returning to the castle, returning to Alice, was the right choice.

CHAPTER 22

"Miss Sharpe?"

Alice looked up from the sketchbook in her lap to find Lord Farleigh coming through the willow tree.

Her heart fell. She had hoped Rupert called to her, though she knew at once the voice was wrong. Rupert's voice was deeper than the young earl's.

Lady Isabelle and Lady Rosalind sat upon the bench on either side of her, both sketching the scene before them as she did. They were at the sunken pool. Lord James lay in the grass nearby, chin in hand, reading a book about the Spanish Armada.

"My lord." She rose to offer a proper greeting, but he waved a hand to dismiss that notion. Alice sank back onto the bench.

Lord Farleigh had said little to her upon their initial meeting the morning before. Though he had apologized for the behavior of his guest and assured her Mr. Briant's welcome had ended.

The heir to the dukedom was in appearance much like his father, almost regal in appearance, though some might find his nose a little too long for the usual standards of attractiveness.

"I have come with guests." He gestured behind him as several giggling children followed from beneath the willow tree. "Lord Addington has arrived." Miss Finchley, the baron's daughter, appeared at the rear of the party, her usual sour expression replaced by a simpering mein.

"Ah. Miss Finchley." Alice hastily repeated her attempt at a curtsy, completing it this time. A baron's daughter would think it her due for the governess to pay such respect.

Miss Finchley's younger siblings, two boys and a girl, along with Geoffrey, were immediately greeted with pleasure.

"We were in the neighborhood," Miss Finchley said, swaying her hips more than strictly necessary as she came to stand next to Lord Farleigh. "My father simply had to stop to speak to His Grace."

Given that the baron's family had attended a house party little more than a week previous, the timing of an unexpected visit likely had more to do with the news the heir had returned. The tight smile Lord Farleigh wore bore further testament to Alice's reasoning.

"Unfortunately, our governess was unwell." Miss Finchley affected a pretty pout. "Crowded carriages do not agree with her."

It had taken the baron's governess half a day to recover from their previous visit.

"Oh, the poor dear." Alice adjusted her spectacles, sliding them further up the bridge of her nose. "I completely understand, and I am happy to mind the children until she feels well again."

Lord Farleigh's relieved smile spoke more of his character than he likely knew. That an earl, son of one of the most powerful men in the kingdom, concerned himself over a governess gave her great hope for the future of the duke's title. How had a family of such prestige remained humble amid the vanity of the noble class?

Miss Finchley cooed and looped her arm more tightly through his lordship's. "Wonderful. Now, my lord, you must show me the portrait gallery as you promised."

As they withdrew, Alice had to admire Miss Finchley's ambition. Most would deem the daughter of a baron beneath the interest of an earl, particularly one set to inherit a dukedom. With a shrug, Alice turned her attention to the children under her care. "Why don't we play a game?" she proposed.

With great enthusiasm, the children proposed hide-and-seek.

Alice had to laugh while she shook her head. "Oh, given the size of the gardens and castle, I am not certain that's a good idea. I know I might well become lost before anyone might find me. Why not blind man's bluff?"

"What shall we use for a blindfold?" Geoffrey asked.

Alice loosened the fichu she wore, made of a thin cream cotton. She folded it over on itself a few times, then held it up for their examination. "This will do, I think. But we cannot play here. Someone might tumble into the little pond. Come, to the meadow."

The children followed after her, speaking excitedly. Lord James had the first turn, running and grasping after the others until he caught one of the Finchley girls.

They repeated the play with laughter, until everyone had been caught except Alice. Though many a governess might consider the game beneath their dignity, she welcomed the distraction.

What better way to soothe her heart than with the laughter of children?

"Miss Sharpe, you must be the blind man." Lord James held the improved blindfold out to her. "Everyone else has had a turn."

"Yes, Miss Sharpe!"

"You cannot catch us if you try!"

Alice crossed her arms. "You think not? But none of you have caught *me*." She looked to her oldest charges, ready to laugh with them over the antics of the younger children.

She saw Lady Rosalind elbow her sister and point back

toward the castle. Eyebrows raised, Alice started to turn to see what had captured their attention.

"Miss Sharpe!" Isabelle practically shouted, startling everyone. "It is most unfair that you will not take a turn."

"Yes, you must put the blindfold on," Lady Rosalind insisted. "If we cannot catch you, you cannot be too worried about catching us."

"I think she's scared," the little Finchley boy chimed in.

Geoffrey glowered at him. "Miss Sharpe isn't scared of anything. Remember when she helped me after I fell out of the tree? She's brave."

The sudden championing from Geoffrey broke through the last of her reluctance. She bent in half. "Very well, children. I will take a turn." She bent forward to allow Lady Rosalind to tie the blindfold about her head. At least she had already discarded her bonnet at the beginning of playing, as had the young ladies.

"Spin her around," Lady Isabelle instructed. "Then follow me!"

Alice spun, Lady Rosalind's hands on her shoulders to keep her from stumbling. "Oh, that isn't fair, all of you banding together."

The children all giggled.

"Because you are so much better than us at the game," Lady Rosalind added, "you must count to ten instead of five."

"All these rules," Alice protested with a laugh. "Very well, I'm counting. One—" She heard squeals of laughter as the children ran. "Two." Their footfalls on the grass withdrew in a hurry. She sped up her count. "Three. Four. Five. Six. Seven." Someone still hovered nearby, or so the sound of grass brushing against boots told her. "Eight. Nine. Ten!"

Alice lunged toward the footfalls she had heard, hands reaching out for small shoulders.

Encountering, instead, a broad chest.

A strong arm encircled her waist.

A deep, warm, and familiar voice whispered in her ear, "You caught me."

"*Rupert!*"

HE HADN'T EVEN CHANGED OUT OF HIS TRAVEL CLOTHES. Nor had he searched out his host first. Rupert had gone directly to the schoolroom, only to find a cross Miss Felton seated at a table sipping at tea.

"I suppose you are after Miss Sharpe," the woman said, nose wrinkled. "I am told she is in the gardens."

Although that was hardly more helpful than saying "she is out in the world somewhere," given the size of the estate, Rupert thanked the woman and rushed from the house.

An undergardener pointed him to the area with the sunken pool, where several discarded bonnets and sketchbooks gave him a hint that the governess had led the children to more wild climes.

He had come to the edge of the meadow, watching as children ran and shrieked in a game of blind man's bluff.

He had started to approach when they stilled, obviously discussing their game. He had aimed for Alice, her tall, lithe figure at the center of the play.

Excitement climbed through his entire body, making his heart sing like a cricket and his stomach leap.

Then they blindfolded Alice, and Rupert nearly stopped.

Until a grinning Lady Isabelle waved him forward.

Bless her little matchmaker's heart.

When the children scampered away, back to the sunken pond garden, Rupert approached Alice more slowly. She was stunning, poised for her run, wearing the same beautiful peach colored gown he had seen her in before.

When her hands landed upon his chest, he instinctively pulled her closer.

"You caught me." Those words held a world of meaning he would have to think upon later.

"*Rupert!*"

She ripped away the bit of cloth covering her eyes, sending her spectacles tumbling from her face as she stared up at him.

He laughed, catching them before they could fall to the ground, keeping one arm securely around her. Then he settled them on the bridge of his own nose, hooking one of the ends behind his ear. "These are useful. Look at that—I can see every one of your beautiful freckles on your nose."

She wrinkled that nose and narrowed her eyes at him. "Rupert, where have you been? And you oughtn't to notice a lady's freckles. Oh, and unhand me before the children see!" She suddenly looked about, her shoulders tensing until she realized they were quite alone.

"I think they have given up your game in favor of another." He bent closer, unable to resist drawing nearer to her. "Why shouldn't I notice your freckles? They are adorable."

Her cheeks turned a lovely shade of pink, and her body relaxed in his hold. "Rupert." She glowered at him, but there was no real heat in the glare. "Why did you leave?"

"You didn't receive my note? I know it was somewhat impersonal, I explained my father called me home. His letter sounded like an emergency, but it wasn't—"

"I never had a note. Only the flowers and sketches."

"Oh." Rupert sucked in a breath. "Alice, you must have thought I abandoned you without word. I put the note in the flowers. I thought for certain you would see it there. I am sorry."

Her smile returned, slowly like a sunrise, until her countenance had brightened. "You were so sincere before. I will admit, there was a moment when I thought you had left because you regretted what you said." She moved closer and tucked her head beneath his chin. "I hoped you would come back. At the very least because I hold several of your sketches hostage."

A laugh escaped him at her unexpected quip. Rupert kissed the top of her forehead while a golden curl stirred against his cheek. "I will prove myself to you, Alice. One day at a time. I will never abandon you."

"Even if we do not suit one another?" she asked, voice soft as the brush of a butterfly wing.

How could he ever reassure her? Too many people had ignored her, cast her aside, put her at the edges of their lives and affection. Alice deserved so much more.

Rupert meant to give it to her.

"I have never met a woman who suits me as you do. It will be me, not you, Alice, who may be found wanting." He closed his eyes, noting the rightness of how it felt to hold her. "I am a man of few interests, I obsess over ants and dandelion puffs, and I discard the conventions of Society whenever it is convenient to me. How could anyone put up with such a man?"

"Quite easily when he notices things like freckles and calls them *adorable*." She lifted her head and placed a kiss at the corner of his jaw. How the subtle touch could make his heart thrum with the intensity of thunder, Rupert did not know. Perhaps there were some things science could not explain.

He placed a hand to her cheek, tilting her gently into the perfect position to bestow a kiss upon her that left him both satiated and wanting much, much more.

Alice sighed against his lips as he withdrew.

"Alice, I have given it some thought. With your permission, I should like to ask His Grace if it might be possible to bend the rules which govern your position. I do not want to court you in secret. I want everything to be above reproach."

To his great relief, she smiled rather than withdraw. Her eyes gleamed up at him before she raised both hands to carefully remove her spectacles from his face. She settled them on her nose, adjusting the hooks behind her ears.

"I have seen the duke's kindness for myself. If you promise I can be present when you inform him of your intentions to a woman in his employment, I give my consent. But Rupert." She lowered her voice to a whisper. "I am fairly certain kissing a woman to whom you are not betrothed is already skirting a great many rules."

He laughed and kissed her again.

CHAPTER 23

Alice returned to the sunken pond, where the children had started skipping stones across the little pool to see if anyone's rock might make it to the other side. On Rupert's arm, she blushed at the knowing grins of Lady Isabelle and Lady Rosalind. Rupert took his leave of their party.

"It would be terribly rude of me if I did not inform the duke of my return." He gave Alice's hand a last squeeze before leaving.

She watched him go, feeling all was right with the world for the first time since she had lost her parents. She turned to her charges. "Lady Isabelle, Lady Rosalind." They approached, their smiles turning more hesitant. Alice relieved their doubt with a laugh. "Thank you for looking after the children in my absence."

"Of course, Miss Sharpe," Lady Isabelle said, tucking her hands behind her back most demurely. "Did you enjoy the end of the game?"

Lady Rosalind giggled and slapped a hand over her mouth.

"Perhaps I will answer that question later. When you are both much older." Alice waved them back to their friends, then settled with her sketchbook in hand again.

She herded all the children back to the schoolroom for their small dinner, but everyone except Lady Isabelle and Lady Rosalind asked to go outside again to enjoy the cool of the evening before darkness settled on them.

"The baron and his family are invited to join the duke for dinner," Miss Felton said, shaking her head over the disturbance in her routine. "I suppose we are to stay until nightfall. Perhaps if the children tire themselves adequately, we will have some peace in the carriage when we return to the Addington estate."

"A good thought, Miss Felton." Alice rose from her chair, ready to seek out her bonnet again.

"Oh, no need. You had them all of the afternoon." Miss Felton rose, her pinched expression easing. "I suppose I could do with some evening sun before I am boxed up again, too. Come children."

Lord James cast Alice a somewhat disappointed glance, but he, Geoffrey, and three of the baron's children followed Miss Felton out the door. Alice fell back into her chair, most relieved. She picked up the book she had been meaning to finish, allowing the older girls to practice the art of conversation with their remaining friend.

But her mind wandered, again and again, to Rupert's return. His kiss. His adoration of her freckles. Merely allowing herself to think of him made her toes curl in her shoes and her cheeks grow warm. His affection had not waned. He had not left because of her.

Where could his note of explanation have gone?

Alice looked to where the faded blooms still stood in their vase near one of the wide schoolroom windows. She rose and went to inspect the blooms. Really, she ought to have allowed the maid to remove them the day before, but she had been hesitant to lose the last blooms Rupert had sent to her. Even if they were sent for science, rather than sentiment.

They were from him. That had been enough.

"Miss Sharpe, will you play Whist with us?" Lady Rosalind

asked. "Mabel doesn't know how to play very well. We need to help her practice."

Alice put the vase down and gave her full attention to the girls. "Of course. I would be delighted to help you, Miss Mabel. Will you be my partner?"

The schoolroom darkened as they played, and a maid entered to see to the fire and light more lamps. Alice barely noticed the passing time before the door opened, with Miss Felton leading the children back into the room. Alice glanced up from her hand of cards and greeted them with a smile.

"Did all of you enjoy your play?"

Lord James slouched into a chair near the door, scowling. "We were playing hide-and-seek."

"Oh?" Alice looked to see the Addington children appeared unbothered, clamoring as they did to eat the last of the biscuits from dinner. She looked to Miss Felton. "Did something go amiss during the game?"

Miss Felton's sour expression was back. "Geoffrey went amiss." She sniffed and leaned over Miss Mabel's shoulder. "Play that one, dear."

The girl followed the governess's instruction and won the trick for herself and Alice.

"Where is Geoffrey?" Alice asked, realizing he had not come in with the others. His mop of curly hair wasn't even peeking around the doorway. When Miss Felton only sniffed, Alice fixed her gaze on Lord James. "Where is he?"

He pointed an indignant finger at Miss Felton. "*She* wouldn't let me find him."

Alice rose from the table, letting her hand of cards drop to its surface. "Miss Felton?"

"That boy is nothing but troublesome. He is full of mischief and of a poor temperament. That is what comes from being orphaned. No natural parents to keep him in check."

Alice felt the eyes of Lady Isabelle, Lady Rosalind, and Lord

James upon her. The baron's children were oblivious to the storm rising in her breast, but apparently her charges knew.

"Miss Felton. Geoffrey is a *child* under your care. That you could leave him alone in a strange place, with night coming on, says more about *your* lack of compassion than his character. An orphan he might be, but that makes him no less worthy of care or attention. I will bring this matter before the duke and duchess, *after* I have found Geoffrey."

Alice went to the door, snatching up a lamp with a handle as she went. The small lantern would have to do. "Lord James?" she asked as she went to the doorway.

He jumped to his feet. "We were playing in the meadow, by the woods."

Though Alice's center went cold, she gave a tight nod and left the room, shutting the door behind her.

She went directly to the nearest doors to the garden, on the ground floor of the house. As she passed the dining hall, hearing sounds of laughter and conversation inside, she hesitated.

There wasn't a moment to lose.

Even if the woods terrified her.

Would anyone at the duke's table care that a boy had gone missing, or would they see it as her duty to return him without causing a fuss?

She put her lantern on a table and drew in a deep breath. No one had fought for her, ever. She had been left in the woods for hours as a child, because her negligent relatives thought she would find her way home when she was hungry enough or frightened enough. A groundsman had finally come looking for her—an older servant with grandchildren she had played with a time or two.

Geoffrey deserved better from Alice.

She entered the dining room without knocking and strode several steps inside before she faltered.

The duke and duchess sat at either end of their fine table. The baron, his wife, eldest daughter, the earl, and Lady Josephine were all eating and enjoying their meal and wine.

Rupert sat with his back to her, but he turned before anyone else knew she was there.

And stood. "Miss Sharpe."

The room fell quiet. Alice kept her gaze locked with Rupert's and did not dare to look at anyone else. Her whole frame trembled at the brazenness of her actions, and she hid her trembling fingers behind her back. The duke had proven kind when his guest attacked her, but would he look upon her interruption of a formal meal with the same care?

"Geoffrey is missing. He might be lost in the woods."

Rupert left the table and was by her side immediately. "How long has he been gone?"

Alice lifted her gaze to his. "Not long. He is all alone."

"Gregory." The Duchess beseeched her husband, and Alice saw the duke already on his feet.

"We will search for him at once."

His son rose from his chair beside Miss Finchley, tossing his napkin to the table.

Miss Finchley's high-pitched whine brought everyone to a halt. "This cannot be necessary. He will find his way back."

Alice's chest tightened.

"Miss Finchley," the duke said, voice stern. "He is a child. Not a dog. I should not have him frightened one moment longer than necessary." The expression on the duke's face was not disgust, but certainly disapproval.

"Come, Alice." Rupert took her hand, leading Alice from the room.

"The lantern—" She pointed to the table, and Rupert scooped it up. "We aren't waiting for the others?"

"We will go to the stables and mobilize the grooms. The duke will want this organized, not all of us spilling out into the night to get as turned around as the boy." Rupert cast her a reassuring smile. "We will find him, Alice. He will hear all of us calling for him."

She hoped he was right.

RUPERT'S OPINION OF HIS HOST IMPROVED THAT EVENING. When the Duke of Montfort organized the search party, it took him less than five minutes to make his plans clear. He divided the grooms and under-gardeners still at the castle, and all the footmen, into groups of two, giving one man in each pair the task of carrying a lantern.

Then the duke had looked at Rupert and Alice's joined hands. His Grace's eyebrows rose, but he said nothing. He claimed his son as a partner and took the center path. Everyone spread out, a distance of ten feet apart, and entered the woods, calling for the little boy.

Geoffrey's name echoed between the trees, and lights drifted in the darkness like fireflies.

"Geoffrey!" Alice shouted, her clear voice a bell among the deeper tones of the men. "Oh, Rupert, I hope he has not gone far, or hurt himself. What if he tried to climb another tree?"

"We will find him, Alice." Rupert held the lamp aloft and shouted the boy's name into the night.

It felt like they searched for hours, walking through the woods in a straight line, until someone nearby whistled and shouted.

"We found him! Your Grace, we found him!"

"Thank heavens," Alice cried, releasing Rupert's hand in order to lift her skirts. She jumped over woodland debris, with Rupert close behind her. A gardener and footman stood together beneath a tree, lantern held high, looking up into the branches.

Alice stepped between them, looking up as well. "Geoffrey. Oh, sweet boy, you're safe."

Rupert came up behind her. The boy clung to a branch nine

feet from the ground, his face white and streaked with dirt and tears.

"I-I-I was hiding, and I got-got lost." Then his voice grew softer. "Am I in trouble?"

"No, dear." Alice looked to Rupert. "Can you catch him?"

He handed her the lantern. "I can. You men, call off the search. We will fetch him down and go back to the castle. Be certain the duke is informed."

The footman nodded and the gardener tipped his cap, then they went in opposite directions, shouting that the boy was safe.

"Geoffrey, do you remember me? Mr. Gardiner?"

The boy nodded. "Yes, sir."

"I am going to stand beneath you. I want you to try climbing down, but if you fall, I will catch you. I promise."

The boy sniffled and nodded, his little face adopting a brave expression. Slowly, the boy stretched his foot to a lower branch. He uncurled one arm most reluctantly from where it clung. Then he moved down a little more, and he managed to lower himself two feet before he slipped.

Rupert caught him easily, then held the child close a moment. The poor mite shook all over with fear and exhaustion. Alice relieved Rupert of Geoffrey to hug him tightly to her chest.

"I was so worried," she said quietly. "When you didn't come back to the schoolroom, Lord James told me you were missing."

"I didn't mean to get lost." The boy held her tight, then he started to cry. "I'm sorry. Is Miss Felton angry?"

Rupert's heart broke in two. The horrid, frosty governess ought not be allowed to look after anyone's children if the boy's greatest concern was raising her ire.

"The duke is not angry at you," he said stoutly. "And his opinion matters most. He organized this entire search party for you, after Miss Sharpe told him you were in the woods."

"The duke?" The boy fairly squeaked the title.

Alice nodded somberly, then took a handkerchief from her

sleeve to wipe at the child's cheeks and beneath his nose. "Come. I know he will want to see you safe for himself."

She took one hand, Rupert took the other, and they brought Geoffrey out of the woods.

A memory came to Rupert, of Alice shuddering at the very sight of the trees, and in broad daylight. "Do you know, Geoffrey, that Miss Sharpe is quite afraid of the woods?"

She gave him a quick glance.

"She is?" the boy whispered.

"Yes. She came into them anyway, because she cares about you." Rupert met her eyes in the dim light of the lantern. "And I love that she would do such a thing. I hope, someday, she might care for me that way."

The boy actually sounded amused. "Lady Isabelle says she thinks Miss Sharpe is going to marry you."

Rupert laughed. "Only if I am very, very fortunate."

"It sounds as though I ought to have a word with Lady Isabelle about gossip." Though she tried to sound unamused, Rupert could hear her smile in her voice.

"And Lord James says you'd better not marry her," Geoffrey continued, between sniffles.

Alice sucked in a deep breath.

"Why would Lord James say that?" he asked quietly, meeting Alice's gaze above the boy's head.

"Because he doesn't want her to go away. I don't blame him. Miss Sharpe is too nice to get married."

Rupert gave the boy's hand a squeeze. "Don't you know, lad? The nicest ladies make the very best of friends. And wives. Now, why don't you tell me about your tree climbing? You seem to enjoy the sport."

Alice remained silent during the rest of their walk.

When they arrived at the castle stables, most of the search party had returned, with more streaming in. Geoffrey's eyes widened again at the crowd of men gathered, and several of them either nodded or winked in his direction.

"All these people were looking for me?" he asked, voice soft amid the many footsteps on the gravel and stone.

Before Rupert or Alice could answer, the duke's voice rang through the stable yard. "Here is our adventurer. Master Geoffrey."

The crowd parted and bowed as His Grace approached the boy, Lord Farleigh at his side. Alice sunk into a curtsy, Rupert bowed, and Geoffrey hastily followed suit.

"Are you well, Master Geoffrey?"

"Y-yes, sir," the child whispered.

"Yes, Your Grace," Alice corrected gently.

"Yes, Your Grace."

The duke went down on his knee before the boy. "I am glad to hear it. All of us must happen upon misadventure occasionally. The important thing is that we learn from it and try not to repeat our mistake. Do you understand?" His tone was gentle, precisely the sort a man ought to use with a child.

Geoffrey, overwhelmed and exhausted, nodded mutely.

"Simon." The duke stood and motioned his son forward. "Why don't you take Master Geoffrey to the kitchens and let them spoil him a bit. Every adventure ought to end with warm milk and a biscuit."

The earl chuckled. "Nearly all of mine did at his age." Then he held his hand out to Geoffrey. "Come along, Master Geoffrey. Cook will know just what you need." With a trust born of exhaustion, Geoffrey put his hand in the much larger one of the duke's son, then the two of them walked to the house.

The rest of the men began returning to their duties.

Why put off for another moment the thing which weighed most upon Rupert's mind? Rupert put his arm around Alice's waist and tucked her close to his side. "Your Grace, I realize this might be odd timing, but might we speak with you a moment?"

Alice did not argue and instead tipped her head back enough to smile up at him.

The duke chuckled and folded his hands behind him. He raised one dark eyebrow and looked from Rupert to Alice with an amused twinkle in his eye. "Of course. I should very much like to know why my entomologist and governess appear to be on such close terms."

For a moment, Rupert felt Alice tense at his side. As brave as she had become, he did not blame her one whit for her nervousness in that moment.

"Through our work on the catalog, Your Grace," Alice answered the question, her tone conveying respect and the slightest hesitancy to speak. "But things have advanced, you might say."

Rupert hurried to add, "To the point that I should like to court Miss Sharpe, with Your Grace's permission."

Rupert held his breath, and Alice did the same.

"My permission?" The duke chuckled. "Miss Sharpe is of age. If she gives her consent, I give mine."

Rupert released a shaky laugh. "You do? I mean—thank you, Your Grace."

"I expect everything to be conducted as becomes a gentleman and lady, of course. Miss Sharpe, should you require a chaperone, Miss Arlen might be willing to provide her company. And"—he held up a finger to underscore his point—"your duties must be fulfilled to the standard you promised the duchess."

"Yes, Your Grace." Alice released Rupert and sank into a low curtsy. "Thank you, for everything. I promise I will continue to make your children my priority, Your Grace."

"Unless you decide to accept Mr. Gardiner." The duke sighed deeply. "At which point, we will need to find a new governess. Again." He gestured to the castle. "I am certain we are too late to enjoy dinner, but perhaps you would both join me in my study? I can have some food brought up from the kitchens, and we can discuss the estate catalog. How close do you think we are to completion, Gardiner?"

Rupert took Alice by the arm, the two of them following the duke into the castle together. To his delight, Alice shared her impressions of the work, and the three of them conversed with ease on their interest of the natural world.

With his courtship of Alice approved by the Duke of Montfort, Rupert promised himself he would succeed.

How could he ever find someone as intelligent, lovely, and compassionate as Alice Sharpe?

She interrupted his musings just before they climbed the stairs. "Oh, Rupert, you have a spider on your shoulder. Probably from the woods." She rose and used her bare hand to scoop up the creature and hurried back to the door, where a bemused footman opened it again for her to let the spider free on the front steps.

"I think," the duke whispered to Rupert as he watched the governess, "you had better marry that one."

When Alice turned, her smile in place and her blue eyes shining with happiness, Rupert could only nod. "I intend to, Your Grace. As soon as she will agree to it."

ALICE ENTERED THE CHILDREN'S WING QUITE LATE, AND SHE found Lord James waiting for her. He sat on the floor in front of her door, leaning against it. When she stood before him, a lamp in hand, he sat up and rubbed at his eyes.

"Geoffrey said you saved him," the boy said, his tone subdued.

"Mr. Gardiner and I helped him down from the tree and walked him to the castle. But there were a lot of people looking for him." She lowered herself to the floor, sitting beside him. "You did the right thing when you told me he was missing, Lord James. Thank you for that."

The boy raised his gaze to hers, and she saw the brightness of tears in his eyes. "I don't always do the right thing, though. I did something very wrong, Miss Sharpe."

She studied him, even while her heart ached for the little boy. He was still so young, yet bore a great responsibility merely for being born to a duke and duchess. "What have you done, darling? I am certain it is not too terrible. We can set it to right."

His bottom lip quivered a moment, then he lifted his chin. "I hid the note Mr. Gardiner left for you. I saw it in the flowers, the day he left. Isabelle said you'd probably leave us to marry him, and I didn't want you to g-g-go." A sob broke from him on the last word, and he buried his face in his hands.

This missing note explained, and the thief's confession, filled Alice with relief. She wrapped the little boy in her arms and held him tight. "It was very wrong to take it, Lord James." He nodded against her. "I want you to know, though, that I forgive you."

He pulled back and looked up at her, his eyes wide. "You do? I thought you'd hate me."

"I could never hate you, Lord James. You see, I like you very much. Even if I go away, that will never change."

His shoulders relaxed and he nodded, then wiped at his tears with the back of his hand. "What will happen to Geoffrey? Miss Felton is a horrid—"

"*Lord James.*" Alice fixed him with a stern expression. "Mind your manners."

"Yes, Miss Sharpe." He lowered his gaze to the carpet on the floor.

She sighed and put her arm around his shoulder again. "I understand your concern. Your father feels the same as you do. The duke has decided to take a special interest in Master Geoffrey. I would not be surprised if he finds a way to bring Geoffrey here to stay at the castle."

Lord James smiled, the expression small and slight. "Papa likes looking after people."

"He does. I think, if you're very good, you may grow up to be just like him." Alice hugged the boy one more time. "Now, you had better go to bed."

She stood, and Lord James slowly followed suit. Then he looked up at her one more time. "I really am sorry, Miss Sharpe."

"Thank you for that. We needn't speak of it again, so long as you behave better from now on." Alice smiled kindly, relieved when he smiled back. "Off to bed with you."

The boy went down the hall to his door, shutting it behind him.

Alice entered her room and prepared for bed, her heart lighter than it had been in a very long time.

EPILOGUE

Although Alice had waited patiently for the better part of the summer, she was nearly beside herself with anxiety when the first day of autumn arrived—and with it, the first copy of Rupert's catalog.

The master copy, meant for the duke's library, with all the original illustrations colored by her hand.

Alice stood in the library, a grand room with shelves two floors high, with sliding ladders as the only means of reaching the very top shelves. It was one of Alice's favorite rooms in the castle. On a row of chairs facing a tall pedestal, crafted especially for the occasion to hold the bound catalog, sat the ducal family.

The duchess, dowager duchess, Lord Farleigh, Lady Josephine with Miss Arlen, Lady Isabelle, Lady Rosalind, and Lord James, all waited in their seats.

His Grace, Rupert, and Alice stood at the pedestal.

"After six months of your efforts, Mr. Gardiner and Miss Sharpe, it gives me great pleasure to see the fruits of your labors at last. This catalog of the flowers and insects inhabiting our lands will be a marvel for years to come, and through the change of seasons. Who knows but that a century from now, these very pages will be used by the naturalists of the future, to compare their world to ours?" The duke touched the large, green leather cover with reverence. "Thank you for your dedication, both of you, for making this work of science also a work of art."

Then he opened the book and gestured for Alice and Rupert to look at its pages.

Alice noted a ribbon had been placed at the location where the duke opened the pages, and then she realized the significance of the illustration.

"Narcissus," she said softly, her fingertips hovering over the page. "And *Pieris napi*. The little white moth." They had been among her first of his drawings to color in, the flower and creature the first of each they ever discussed.

The room grew very still, and Rupert took her by the hand.

Alice turned and saw him kneeling beside her, and her eyes immediately filled with tears.

"Alice Sharpe, I always thought a book like this one would be my greatest work. The way I would prove myself to the world. But it has done something much more than that—it has brought me you, the one woman in the world who can love me even while I'm elbow-deep in brambles attempting to catch a wasp."

A rather soggy laugh burst from her. That *had* been a memorable occasion.

"I love you, Alice. With His Grace's permission, I would have you as my wife, and my partner, and the mother of my children. Will you have me?"

"Yes. Oh, Rupert. I love you."

He stood quickly and wrapped his arms around her, bending to kiss her soundly on the lips.

"Dear me, in front of the children?" The dowager's disapproval made everyone laugh.

"Oh, Grandmama," Lady Rosalind protested. "It's *romantic*."

Alice and Rupert parted, and the children cheered for her. Until Lord James stopped suddenly. "Wait a moment. Does this mean Miss Sharpe cannot be our governess anymore?"

"I'm afraid so, dear." The duchess smiled kindly at Alice. "But I do believe we will see more of the new Mrs. Gardiner in due time."

Alice leaned against Rupert, resting her head upon his shoulder. Finally, she had a home. She had not expected to find it where she had—in Rupert's arms.

EMMA ARLEN REMAINED IN HER CHAIR WHEN THE CHILDREN and Josephine rose to give their good wishes to Mr. Gardiner and Alice. She watched, as she often did, from the edge of the spectacle, enjoying it even though she did not directly take part.

Like her, Alice Sharpe was an orphan, and she had finally found her place, and a family who loved her.

When the duke and duchess had given Emma a home in their castle, the paint still wet on the day Emma entered the impressive residence for the first time, she had felt rather like a princess. A decade later, only a year away from reaching the requisite age to receive the inheritance her parents left her, she still counted her blessings.

Josephine rejoined Emma on the chairs. "Isn't it marvelous? I hope they will have the wedding in our chapel. It is so dull to only use it for Sunday sermons."

"I do love weddings." Josephine folded her hands in her lap. "Perhaps we can persuade Alice to use it."

"Soon, too. Though I do not suppose Papa will offer to procure them a special license." Josephine raised her eyebrows to suggest she wasn't at all serious. "He will be far too occupied with the ambassador in the coming weeks."

"The ambassador?" Emma blinked at her dearest friend, confused. "Which ambassador? Not that horrid Russian, I hope. His mustaches." She shivered. "I tell you, I saw them dripping with soup after dinner that first evening."

Josephine wrinkled her nose. "Most certainly *not* the Russian. No, this one is from Sicily. Or Milan? I cannot remember. Somewhere in Italy." She waved away the details. "Papa told me I must be on my best behavior. You *know* what that means."

"A bachelor." Emma did not bother to hide her smile. "Poor Josephine."

"I have no wish to marry anyone at the moment." Josephine glowered at Emma. "But if he is very handsome, I might let you try flirting with him."

Emma shook her head and nodded to where Mr. Gardiner and Alice now stood in discussion with the duchess and dowager, while the duke turned the pages in the new book. "I want what they have. Love. I doubt an Italian diplomat would care all that much for the companion to a lady. Not when the lady herself is present."

"We shall see." Josephine folded her arms and leaned back in her chair, a gleam of mischief in her eyes. "Someone will catch your eye one day, my dearest friend. I only hope I am present to congratulate him on the feat."

They laughed together, and then Emma wandered over to the large globe the duke kept in the library. She spun it around on its axis once, then trailed her finger over England, across to France, and down to the boot-shaped mass of land labeled as Italy. She smiled to herself, then gave the globe another spin.

IF YOU ENJOYED THIS GENTLE ROMANCE, MAKE CERTAIN TO read the next in the series, ***A Companion for the Count,*** wherein Emma has a lovely romance of her own.

Another of Sally's stories you might enjoy is ***The Social Tutor***, a gentle story of unintended love.

Sally loves to connect with her readers through her Facebook group and her newsletter. Sign up for either to get all the latest news about releases and other fun!

ABOUT THE AUTHOR

Sally Britton, along with her husband, their four incredible children, and their dog named Izzie, live in Oklahoma. So far, they really like it there, even if the family will always consider Texas home.

Sally started writing her first story on her mother's electric typewriter when she was fourteen years old. Reading her way through Jane Austen, Louisa May Alcott, and Lucy Maud Montgomery, Sally decided to write about the elegant, complex world of centuries past.

Sally graduated from Brigham Young University in 2007 with a bachelor's in English, her emphasis on British literature. She met and married her husband not long after and they've been building their happily ever after since that day.

Vincent Van Gogh is attributed with the quote, "What is done in love is done well." Sally has taken that as her motto, for herself and her characters, writing stories where love is a choice.

All of Sally's published works are available on Amazon.com and you can connect with Sally and sign up for her newsletter on her website, AuthorSallyBritton.com.

Printed in Great Britain
by Amazon